QUILLER'S JOURNAL

SHOYONGDIPTO CHOUDHURY

Made with ❤ on the Notion Press Platform
www.notionpress.com

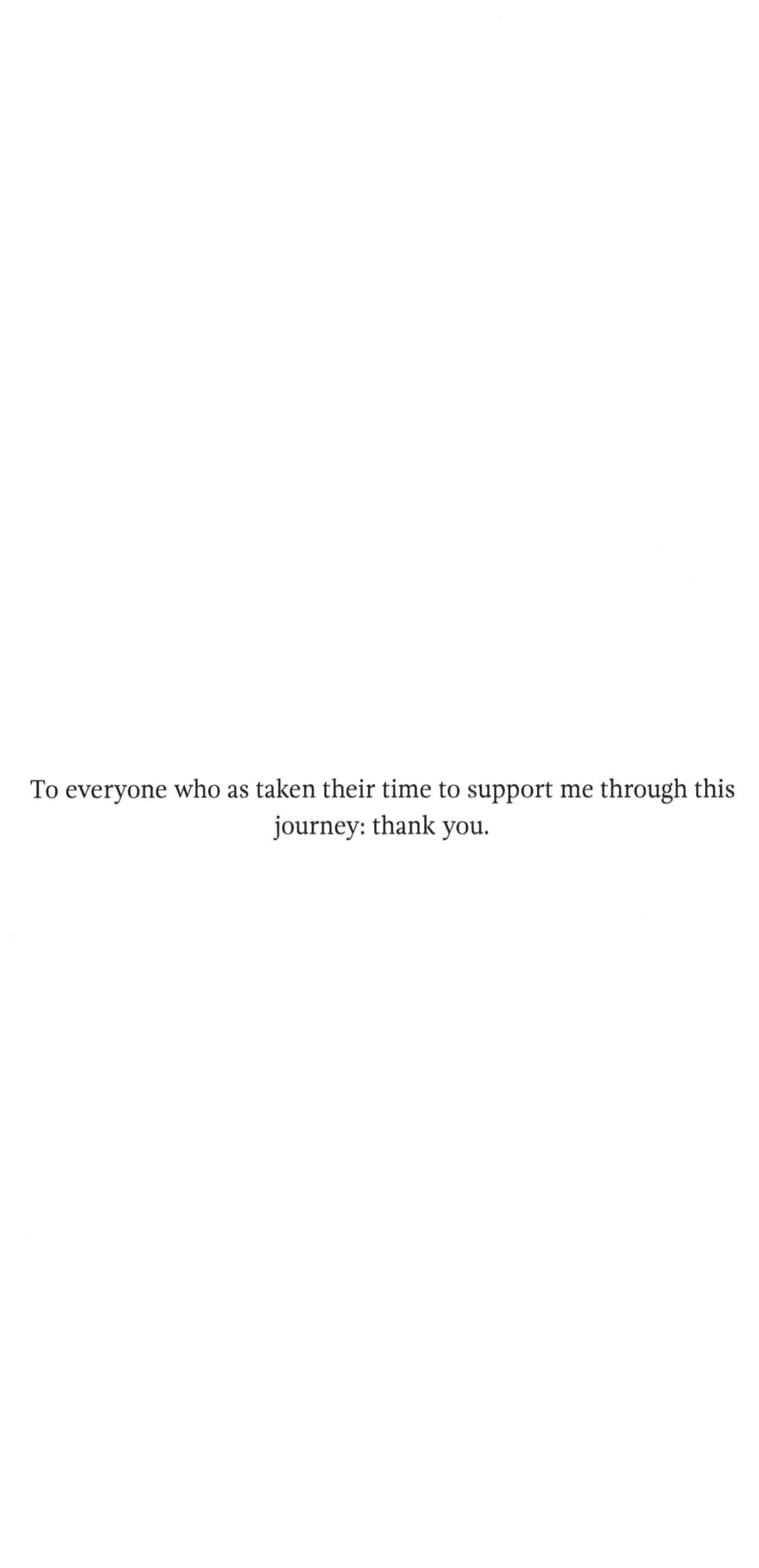

To everyone who as taken their time to support me through this journey: thank you.

Contents

Preface

It never seems easy to do something until you have already done it. That is human nature. For me this book was a product of the same. Throughout my childhood I had always dreamt about being an author, and writing books that could not only engage and entertain the audience, but also invoke a new realisation into anyone, who was kind enough to pick up my book from the bookshelf. Now I feel as though I have done just that. Of course only time will tell, if you truly resonate with my vocation, storytelling, and opinions; I can only hope that you find my work entertaining, however, I know that it will bring out a new realisation within you. A new idea, a new thought, a new dream, I am sure, will sprout out of the soils of your mind, until you yourself have synthesised something brilliant and fantastical into your own life.

I began writing this tale during a time that chose to be harsh. I was met with several difficulties at once, and yet I could not help but sit down in front of my laptop for hours on end-writing. This book found me at a time when I needed support, when I needed a sense of purpose and meaning-and it breathed new life into me as I found a renewed sense of drive and determination. Through this piece of writing, I hope to tell you that life is always going to be unpredictable. Never, even for a fraction of a second, will we be in control. Often times that will hurt, but seldom should it hinder our self image. The spontaneity is what makes it fun, and my characters are here to tell you that through the distress, through frustration, and through the conflicts, life will always bring something to laugh about through its infamously random fashion.

Bonne Chance!

Acknowledgements

To my lovely parents-my first ever audience-who let me stay up on school nights to finish writing this book.
To my sweet grandparents, who took their time reacting critically to my wonky ideas
To my brilliant counsellor and mentor, who inspired me to publish my work.
To my beloved pupper, whose lack pushed me to approach creating something new- Rest In Peace; and keeping wagging your tail all the way to the top of the rainbows.
To the few friends, who kept me sane throughout the writing process.

CHAPTER I

The Chance Meeting

As Hemant walked through the frosty streets of London he looked around. The weather was dreadful. Even after having every inch of his peanut-brown skin covered with thick, woollen clothes, with a huge mask covering his nose and mouth and large glasses protecting his watery pupils from the darting shards of icy wind; he still shivered as he self-diagnosed himself to conclude that he was suffering from hypothermia.

It had been a long day in the hospital and after spending all his time and extensive knowledge on watching an old man cough himself to sleep, instead of saving lives, Hemant had enough. His life was dull...as dull as it ever could have been. Even now, while walking down the bustling city crowd all he saw was shades of grey bumping into each other and apologising over the smallest of matters, laughing potentially for no reason. To Hemant the streets almost looked like a sad bowl of bitter porridge... grey, boring, annoying. Well, a grey bowl of porridge with one distinct black dot. Hemant was suddenly very interested. This silhouette, this figure had an enticing aura around it. Hemant could not at all identify the person's age, gender, or anything about them really. It was just one irregular structure amid the crowd of eternal boredom. Hemant was drawn to this irregular structure, drawn to the tension that it held midst of the 'boring everything'.

He went closer, squeezing himself through the pores of the crowd until he found himself right in front of the abnormal figure. It was a man...a rather young one, a few years younger than Hemant. He had a cigarette pointing towards the smog-filled skies sticking out of his mouth, and with choking smoke spewing out of it. The man wore an expensive trench coat, with the brand name embedded over the right side of the chest, however, that remained to be the only thing that looked remotely fancy about the man.

Under his coat, he sported a shabby white shirt partially tucked out of his plain black trousers, with ink stains all over its un-ironed surface. The man also carried a hand bag with a sub-metallic texture that had a few smudges of crimson.

"It's not tomato sauce." Said the man.

His voice was a mixture of gruff and soft tones which melded together harmoniously. Hemant looked up at the man and noticed his perfectly groomed face...except his hair which shabbily hung over his forehead and scattered to the edges and to the back of his head.

"Huh?" Hemant blurted out. The man had caught him off guard.

"It's not tomato sauce. The stains on my bag. In case you were wondering. "The man said calmly.

"No...erm, I didn't mean to impose..." Hemant began but before he could continue the man spoke again.

"Trust me Dr Shah you aren't imposing at all. I get you. I really do" The man finished, still maintaining his nonchalant demeanour.

"How do you kn..."

"Oh, that's not all. I know that you work at the hospital right around the corner, yes, the one with the terrible washrooms. I know that you are a 30-year-old man, who moved here a few years ago, let's say 5 years ago, from India. You were an intellectual, one of the best in your university and managed to get a scholarship with a cost greater than your parent's salary. After all that you spend your days here as an understudy and you hate it. You are more than capable of doing full-on surgeries yet the residential doctors make you do simple tasks like being a second opinion to a family physician, all out of pettiness. You're simply bored and have been for those five years, and suddenly today while walking through the dull crowds of another dull evening with irritating hypothermia you see an unusual looking man and you're simply interested. Your grey life is the closest to being black and white again and so you decide to come and observe me."

"How did...what... when!" Hemant exclaimed.

The man swiftly took the cigarette out of his mouth and threw it to the ground before drawing a long breath from the air around him.

"There is a slight recession of your hairline that makes your fore-head look a centimetre bigger than average. There's a tinge of white at the edges of your hair and your eye-brows. Your skin, well, whatever of it that is exposed is dry which suggests a smaller concentration of sebum oil on its surface. Your shoes are made of the traditional leather found only in India, however, there are tiny darker spots left on them that suggests there has been snow on those shoes for quite a while now. Also, there is a small tear at the back of the sole suggesting that the shoes are old. The design's old-school which means they were bought a few years back. Ha!... Now I can roughly estimate your age to have been 25 when you came here based on the fashion sense with which the shoes were bought, yet the dark spots suggest you've been here a while. So that would increase the average by a few years, let's say 5 years, which means you are most likely 30. Your dry skin supports that hypothesis, so let's just say 30 and call it a day, eh?"

"Wow...that's incredible!"

"I'm not done. The only time you spoke to me, you pointed your eyes towards the left, you have been holding a pencil in your right hand. You're right-handed and your eyes point towards the left in cognitive correspondence-which we all know means that you're accustomed to utilising the left side of your brain- you're a critical thinker. The pencil you've been holding, it's a completely involuntary action, in fact, you've just realised you were holding it, yet you did it with immense precision denoted by the veins popping out of your wrist. That kind of care only comes when you've operated on bodies with years of experience behind you. However, surgery is an exhilarating task yet here you are observing a random individual for entertainment. Furthermore, your pupils have remained contracted ever since this conversation started even during the small duration of time when you appeared to be fascinated by my deductions. This suggests you are bored most of the time so much so that you've simply stopped dilating your pupils. There's also a slight hint of permanent tension in your glabella that suggests you hate your situation but aren't in a position to change it. Now, based on all that-is it not logical to assume that you're most likely an incredible doctor but also an understudy with insufficient financial aid, I mean if you had money you would probably start practising medicine privately, no? which means your entire higher education was built on scholarships. Your parents not being rich and your mentors being absolute nincompoops was a shot in the dark, but a logical one nevertheless."

"That is simply brilliant! You are-I...don't-I mean- WOW! Y..." Hemant spoke but was interrupted by the man again.

"I know you work at the hospital around the corner, because a set of important documents are hanging out of your shirt pocket, one of them being your Work ID."

"Uh...Haha-do you have a habit of interrupting people a lot?" Hemant asked with an air of irritation around him this time. This, however, was ineffective to the man.

"No, seriously you might want to tuck that back into your pocket; I can see your home address." Said the man earnestly.

"Wait...what, oh uh, no...erm, hold on a minute!" Hemant exclaimed, flustered and embarrassed.

"Oh... you don't believe me," said the man mockingly, "well, does it go like this: 3...7...8....B"

"Shut up, shut up...stop. Alright, it's tucked in. IT'S TUCKED IN!" Hemant paused for a moment to flush out the irritation out of his mind, and upon regaining his calm he asked "Well, what's your name?".

"Quilton Addams" said the man.

"So, Quilton, are you...like a...detective? Maybe a veteran-I mean your skills are quite uncanny...so, uh...help me out here, will you?"

"Detective? Ha! No, I'm not, although I have done that a few times. And uh...I don't have the patience to be in any sort of military sector. OH-NO. No...no doctor, I'm simply a writer."

CHAPTER II

An Intellectual's Game

"A writer?" He asked me, as we sat down in a coffee shop. He had now stopped shaking as the warmth of the hearth in the shop took over the atmosphere. I could notice tiny sweat droplets appearing on his forehead, accumulated at every corner of his creased skin. His eyes remained fixed on me, and he continued to wait, patiently, hoping that I would answer his question. Well, exclamation really, but most people gave me that reaction when I talked about myself. I'm used to it at this point. However, something was different about this one. I could tell. His presence was... complimentary to mine."

"What are you doing on that laptop of yours?" Hemant questioned. As the strange man he had just met typed away rapidly on his laptop, without any concern about the rest of the world.

"Oh...this, well doctor, I told you I write." Said Quilton earnestly.

"Yeah, about that...YOU...you are a...writer?"

"I believe so, yes."

"But then how? How do you know so much about deduction and psychology. How is it possible that such a remarkable individual has no association with the very thing he is brilliant at?" Hemant continued to push his question on to the man, desperate to solve this mystery... to understand what he was dealing with.

"That's where you're mistaken doctor. I do not have a field of specialisation...I specialise in everything."

"Everything?"

"Yes. I'm a remarkable marksman, I like to believe. I have thorough knowledge of almost every subject you could find in the most expensive university, I have won countless medals in different fields of Athletics. I do know the basics of most hand-to-hand combat styles, I am familiar with several fields of natural science especially zoology and botany, and so much more. I probably am as capable as you in medical science."

"You're probably amazing at being a narcissistic, delusional liar too." Said Dr Shah in hushed tones.

"You don't believe me. Well, that's fair enough. I'll prove it to you. Quiz me!" said Addams with utmost confidence and a rather intimidating glare.

"You don't have to ask me twice." Retorted Shah, with the same level of confidence. It was time. He was finally going to test his own intellectual capabilities, face a challenge. The sheer intensity of the moment made Hemant Shah's heart pump halfway out of his chest and he enjoyed every bit of it.

"What's the largest bone in the human body?" questioned Dr Shah.

"Femur." Said Addams immediately.

"How does a numbing agent work?"

"By preventing sodium molecules from attaching to the receptor cells on one's skin," said Addams placidly," doctor you clearly are underestimating m..."

"NAME A NUMBING AGENT!"

"Lidocaine. You may not be good with questions, doctor but you are spectacular at taking the fun out of one of my favourite games." Stated Addams in a playful mocking tone.

"Fine," Hemant now felt his temper rising," you want to play tough, let's play tough!"

"Most commonly used anaesthetic?"

"Propofol."

"Largest part of the brain?"

"Cerebrum."

"Which part of the brain does Heroin affect?"

"The frontal lobe," said Addams, now absolutely engrossed in the game, "have a bit of personal experience with that myself."

"Organ separating lung cavity and chest cavity?"

"Diaphragm, oh come on this is kindergarten stuff!"

It had been a while now. Both the doctor and the writer had started to attract a bit of a crowd, and as they sweated on to the crusty shop rug, due to the now suffocating heat from the hearth,

Dr Shah realised that he was all out of questions. Twilight had finally commenced upon its unfolding, and its presence became more and more evident as the yellow tainted, pollutant-filled sky slowly changed its attire to a darker gown with sparkling jewels embedded in them. Both the men were suddenly brought into their senses when the doctor forfeited, and they realised that they had spent more than an hour in the shop.

"Oh, come on doctor, that can't be all that you've got!" exclaimed the writer.

"No, but I'm a little tired." Lied Hemant. He knew very well that he had met his superior counterpart. The sheer confidence and conviction with which the man named Quilton Addams answered his questions was enough to tell him that this man was a much, much more complex character than what he led people to believe. Hemant did not dare question Quilton from a field of study that was beyond his own comprehension. Addams was already so close to outsmarting Shah in his own field. The hysterical truth that came out of this-pinched right at Hemant's ego; this eccentric man was not even trying. This was a game to Addams, a funny anecdote about which he could write, a small, insignificant event about which he would forget in minutes. Hemant smiled. He had not felt like this in years. This feeling of a pleasant warmth dancing right over his chest, the feeling that told him that he was not alone anymore. He had just met this incomprehensible individual, just about an hour ago, and now there he was indulging in childish fits with the same man. This was the strangest encounter Hemant had ever had in his life, yet it felt like the only one that left him with a friend.

"You know...Addams...this was...somehow-fun. I think I've started to like your company." stated the doctor.

"It's a shame you didn't feel like quizzing me from any other of my preferred sections." Said Addams thickly, "I would have done so well."

"Ok...I'm starting to dislike it a little."

"Well, you might as well get used to it, doctor. You're going to have to put up with it much more often now." Said the writer.

"What do you mean?"

"Well, your acquaintance has been interesting enough for me to start writing about you, and I've already written a good amount. So, I'm not leaving you until the end of this story." Addams explained.

"Well, I am sorry to break it to you mate, but this is life, not a story. It doesn't end for a long time and when it does, it does with you on your deathbed." Said the doctor jokingly.

"All stories end doctor, and life...well, life is just made up of several stories, where one ends another begins."

"Wow...that's actually kind of deep. How'd you come up with th..."

"AND THERE WE GO, FIRST CHAPTER OVER!"

"OK! you've got to learn to stop interu..."

"Bye, doctor, I'll see you when I do." Said the writer, and with that he practically jumped off his seat and ran out of the shop not once turning his head back at Hemant. As the crowd in the shop broke into hushed discussions and laughter, Hemant sat there, trying to understand the situation he had seemingly created for himself.

CHAPTER III

The Masked Man

The cool breeze gently entered through the ajar windows, with crystalline glass and a rusted iron frame, and into Dr Shah's bedroom. The midnight bell had rung several hours ago, and as the first rays of sunlight hit the bedroom walls to create abstract dancing silhouettes on them, Hemant snored away blissfully. The bedroom contained a painting facing the very bed Dr Shah slept on. The bed was stout in nature, with plain white sheets. The floor was hard concrete, cold, and icy at this hour. A few pots of exuberant plants rustled against the wind, on a wooden table next to Shah's bed, and an old, worn-out heater, choked on its own warm air, making unpleasant noises in the background. The bedroom had a door that led to the hallway, and another one that connected Shah's bedroom to his study...the study with brilliant annotations over the several white boards, with diagrams of potential discoveries scrawled onto loose paper, and a few models with dust on them. The floor was fully furnished in the study...it was completely wooden and every spot was clean and clear, contrary to the bedroom. Most of the area on the walls were taken by the white boards, however a few areas remained covered with framed photos of scientists and mathematicians as well as pictures of certain animals that Shah was keen about. The study also had a door which led to the hallway-the most generic of all the rooms. It had plain white walls like the bedroom but not even one painting decorated them. A flatscreen television lay opposite to the only sofa in the hallway. The sofa was pitch black, so much so that the television could not reflect it. A bathroom lay at the corner of the hallway, which faced Shah's bedroom as well. A few cabinets and a tiny kitchen island remained right next to the washroom; however, this was mostly unused as Shah was not the best at cooking.

This was Dr Shah's sanctuary, his haven... and it was soon going to be majorly disrupted-its peace... violated.

"Eagle 1 do you have a visual? a muffled voice spoke into a microphone in the distance.

"Reporting to Alpha, Eagle 1 has visual."

"Copy that Eagle 1, release the falcons for minute perimeter scan."

"Roger that, Alpha. Beta, releasing falcons, do you copy?"

"Copy that Eagle 1, we're ready for ground surveillance."

"Roger that, Beta, initiate ground surveillance."

"Ground surveillance, initiated."

"Eagle 1, prepare for landing."

"Copy that, Alpha, we're ready to land."

"Beta, has surveillance reached autopilot?"

"Beta reporting to Alpha, autopilot has been achieved."

"Copy that. Beta, get into position. Eagle 1, initiate landing."

"Roger that, Alpha."

"Copy that, Alpha."

As this conversation of strange verbatim took place, through muffling microphones, a massive army helicopter, surrounded by a swarm of drones with incomprehensibly advanced technology, landed briskly in front of Hemant's apartment building, which was now surrounded by metal strands with light of several different electromagnetic frequencies projecting out of the top and hitting the drones and the helicopter. The grounded metal devices, standing completely erect, seemed to induce a field around the drones and the giant green flying object that the helicopter was, to prevent any sound from being heard. No one knew what was happening. No one knew that a team of specialists were landing their remote flying craft in the centre of London.

Dr Shah was still asleep, comfortably tucked at the edge of his bed.

BANG! The door to his room fell to the ground, completely unhinged from the several bolts and screws, and as its wooden surface slapped the cold floor, Hemant woke up, looking around, confused. There were several men, most wore armoured attire of those like the marines or swat teams. However, there was a single individual who...stood out. Amid the grey hues of armour plates and huge guns and melee weapons, one man stood there... hands in the pocket of his trench coat, with a complete business attire of expensive branding underneath his coat, and a really strange mask.

"W-who...w-what is h-happening?" Hemant asked, shaking, as fear slowly crept up his spine.

"So, you've reached a first-name-basis, have you?" the man spoke. His voice was deep, but strangely playful.

"What?" Shah spoke, "WHO ARE Y..."

"Watch...your...tone, doctor." The man spoke with a slight tension but still with complete calmness. He silenced Hemant immediately. The doctor-had gotten used to a dull life; this was... too much. This was like a fairy-tale!

"In the next few days, you are going to have many more encounters with the eccentric you've befriended—this...man from the coffee shop." The man spoke," I trust that when I come knocking on your door again, you'll have information for me."

"What d-do you mean? What's he done? What information? WHO ARE Y..." Hemant tried to inquire once more; however, he was again interrupted.

"Quit playing dumb, doctor." the man spoke through the darkened fabric of his mask, "Well...it's not really what he has done, more so, what he is."

"What is he, then?" Dr Shah asked as he regained a sense of confidence and alertness.

"The most dangerous man that you'll ever meet. Well; besides me, of course." The man said playfully. "He is insane, doctor, a threat to the whole world. I presume that deluded piece of..." the masked man caught himself before he could continue, and after a quick breath spoke once more, with a deliberate restraint on his emotions "I presume...that this man that you've befriended told you that he is a 'writer'. Well, he will go to any and all lengths to get 'content' for his writing."

"But..." Hemant tried to protest.

"Well, that'll be all. You've one month and then I'll rid you of the trouble you've caused yourself. BUT... double-cross me...and I'll have your head on my display!"

"W-Who...are you?" Asked Hemant, as he slowly felt his confidence leak out of his body again. The masked man came a little closer to Hemant, and hunched down in front of him, so that Hemant was directly looking at him. The man's mask had one lens drawn out as a monocle with embedded gold on it. He was also wearing a black, short hat. Hemant could feel the hairs on his back stand, as a chill ran down his spine. Even though he knew the man could only see from that one lens, and even though Hemant could not see the man's eyes, he felt it...he felt the man glare at him; and as the man did so, he said:

"I...am a creature of the night... a devil whose existence...is far superior to yours, and whose power...is far beyond your comprehension!"

The sheer intensity of the moment was enough to give Dr Shah a heart attack. He remained completely frozen, shocked by the deathly soft tone with which he was given his final warning. The masked man drew back to his original position, as all the armoured soldiers observed his every move. Even then, in the deepest state of shock and confusion, it was clear to Dr Shah that this anonymous man was the pack leader. He had no gun, not even a pistol with himself, nor was he padded with protective metal plates all over his body, yet there was this tension in Hemant's placid bedroom, that told him that every armoured man in his room would have been devastated if he were to face the masked one. With one swift gesture of his hand, the anonymous masked man commanded the soldiers to abandon the room, and they followed in complete uniformity. As the strange masked individual slowly crept out of the room, he slightly turned his head back, to glare at Hemant once more.

"Consider this your last chance," the man said," to go back to a grey life. Trust me doctor, the black and white is more... dangerous...than interesting." With that the man disappeared into the jagged shadows that stretched into the corridors of Dr Shah's apartment, and before Hemant could register any of this, he heard a distinct click, and then a loud bang that told him that his front door had just been shut from the outside...with extreme vigour.

CHAPTER IV

The Friendly Lunatic

"The sunlight shot like darts and meandered through the chemical smog, to enter my refuge. Through my irregularly shaped windows, it entered to illuminate my possessions: a laptop kept on a worn down, wooden table, with a slender stool behind it, as well as a tiny almirah, with corroded metal doors and a smeared mirror. I lied still on my mattress, well, the landlady's mattress really. It was rather uncomfortable to sleep on and with a dirty beige colour and exposed springs on either side of its surface. The light, signified dawn, the time when all humans are to wake up. The body is a wonder... with each component being of use, down to the last-minute organelle in a single cell. I often try to comprehend what happens in my body at a certain moment in time, it makes emotions easier to go down. Right then, I knew I had a large concentration of adrenaline in my blood stream, making me excited and hopeful... preparing me for my daily activities. The line of work I do, requires a lot... of adrenaline. Well, I had oxytocin too, but that predominantly was to taint the dark line I walk on, with a pleasant white wash. My mind does that a lot, it makes it easier for things to go down. Speaking of 'things going down', I think I'm going to pay my newly found acquaintance another visit, considering the fact that he has known me for more than 3 hours."

Dr Shah slowly opened his eyes. The morning light crept into his bedroom through the translucent windows and reflected against the walls, going everywhere and making dust dance in the air. Hemant could barely open his eyes. He felt this strange rush of anxiety creeping up on him. It was as though he had gone through something inexplicable. May be, it was a dream or may be Hemant was just not thinking straight as he had just woken up; but he kept thinking about the words "grey life" And "black and white" and...

Dr Shah's eyes hopped around the bedroom to glance at every object present and before he knew it, he saw it. His bedroom door lying on the floor...completely broken off the hinges. Suddenly it all came back to him. Dr Shah started shaking in his bed and tensing every muscle in his body. What was even happening? His plain, simple life had turned into a Hollywood movie. Yes, it had been boring and dull since... well, since forever; but at least back then it made sense. Right now, nothing made sense to Shah. He was confused, very...very confused; and Dr Shah hated being confused.

DING...DONG! The bell rang loudly startling Hemant so greatly that he jumped off the bed and fell to the ground. It took Dr Shah a little while to get off the cold, hard floor and as he rubbed his dry palms against his back he walked to the main door. Knowing what his life had turned into, practically overnight, Shah was a little reluctant on opening the door.

Who was that masked man? Was he back? Why did he want to hunt down Quilton Addams? Did that mean that Addams was an international criminal? All those guards...all those soldiers following the one-monocled man's command. It was as though an elite secret task force was after Addams. Could Addams really be that dangerous? What if it was the Queen of England telling Shah that Quilton Addams was a deranged lunatic who had once attempted to steal the crown jewels in order to write a chapter in one of his books? Crazed thoughts raced the neural tracks of Dr Shah's mind and his hand remained on his door knob, unable to make a decision. Eventually, Hemant's irritation caught up to him and he just yanked open the door due to sheer frustration. Good news: it wasn't the queen. Bad news: it was the deranged lunatic himself.

"Toodles doctor! How are you doing? It's a beautiful m..."

Dr Shah slammed the door shut as fast as he had opened it.

"Hey! That's a little mean don't you think, doctor?" said the voice from the other side of the door playfully.

"Just go away, okay?", Exclaimed Hemant, "It'd be better if you just forget about me and I just forget about you!"

"What's gotten into you, doctor?" asked the voice from the other side of the door, still playful, however now, with a tinge of concern.

"My life was fine as it was. I don't need this. I thought I could handle the *white and the black* or whatever you people call it, but I've realized I'm fine with the *grey life*, okay? Please just leave me alone! Please."

"So...you've met him." Said the voice.

"W-What?" asked Hemant shakily.

"He is pretty scary, eh doctor?", said the voice," I can only help you if you let me. You're too deep in this now, might as well embrace it."

Hemant slowly opened the door and as he did, he realized he had started crying. A few teardrops still blurred Hemant's vision but he could still see the strange young man with an expensive branded trench coat, messy over grown hair, a stained and un-ironed Shirt along with trousers, and a sub-metallic bag with more red stains on it.

"It's not tomato sauce, in case you were wonderin'." The young man said smiling comfortingly and Dr Shah found himself smiling back...smiling back at his only friend.

CHAPTER V

A Talk Over Some Tea

The ripples of vibration fostered the reflection of light, making the tea in their cups look a certain way. The acquaintances sat in silence as the day continued to unfold. The writer stared down at his cup of tea and seemed to ponder upon a thought with immense focus. Dr Shah simply sat back, leaning against the spine of his black sofa, attempting to comprehend these last 24 hours of his life. The silence was peaceful, as though somebody had hit the pause button on Dr Shah's life. For the first time, he seemed to be able to appreciate the simplicity of his endeavours, and truly understand, how poorly he would do if his life was remotely exhilarating.

"It's not like that, doctor" The man in the brown trench coat spoke," you're just out of practice."

Dr Shah blinked and stared up at his acquaintance. Just like that, the man in the trench coat had amused Hemant again by reading his mind and going as far as responding to Hemant's thoughts. This time, however, the element of surprise ceased to exist.

"Is it even worth asking, how you did that?" Hemant asked placidly.

The writer smiled." I was simply reading your lips. You seem to have an unconscious habit of silently speaking out everything you think." The writer retorted back. The sun shined brightly and its light hit both the individuals in the face.

"I'm scared Addams. I'm confused. My life has turned into this freaky fairy-tale in the span of a few hours... and I can't make even a penny worth of sense out of any of the incidents. I...I can't tell the difference between reality and dreams, for...! I..."

"Calm down, doctor. When life seems inexplicable, the first step should always be to calm our nerves. Take it from a man who's been living this inexplicable life for a long time." The writer said, finally sipping on his cup of tea. "You know I would have actually preferred coff..." the writer this time was cut off by the doctor.

"Tell...me...everything...please. Explain to me the inexplicable; give me a sense of comfort in knowing something about what has happened and what is about to happen. Please Addams...please." Hemant said with a dramatic halo around his entire presence.

"Alright doctor. However, if you wish to hear a monologue concerning the explanation of what your life has turned into, you shall allow me to speak freely, and never shall you interrupt me-no matter how unconventional, impractical or unbelievable my words seem and no matter how bewildered you become after hearing them. Do we have a deal?" The man in the trench coat asked as he took another sip of his tea.

"I would do anything to make some darn sense out of this nonsense!" words came out of the doctor's mouth with uncontrolled fluidity, the doctor's tongue lubricated by distress.

"Fair enough," the writer continued "for starters, my name is not Quilton Addams. However, you shall call me that for now. Having an overview of what it feels like to be in my shoes, I trust that you have no obligation to my decision of not disclosing my name. Logic would not permit you to do so. I will continue to live my live by dawning several aliases and only when I trust you completely, shall I reveal my real name. This, however, does not mean that I do not trust you. I trust you to a great degree, but still, not enough to give you my name, doctor. I find you very interesting and I will admit that your personality is fairly complementary to mine. Now that I have involved you, my enemies will attempt to get to me-through you! I don't plan on abandoning you, nor do I desire to deliberately put you in danger to ensure my own safety. However, if worse comes to worse I will resort to these heartless methods of survival for I am a man of logic, and I will do whatever...logic permits. Until now, you've only seen my playful side, but the unfortunate truth remains that my occupation requires me to be the most heartless, the cruellest and the most robotic of individuals; it requires me to lead life with sheer precision and critical thinking. I still pity you, doctor. But know that you wouldn't have led a risk-free life even if you hadn't encountered me; this encounter was necessary for reasons that I can only talk about later. Just know that *they* were after you from the very start.

That out of the way, I shall now explain to you, what the current scenario looks like for us.

The man you met last night, may have told you that I'm a very dangerous individual who is eccentric in his ways. He may have also told you that I will go to any lengths to achieve 'content' for my writing. Even though he is partly right, he will always choose to antagonise me to a certain extent, for he opposes me, and to seek me out as his foe he needs to believe that I am the worst thing inflicted upon man-kind. Otherwise, his system of mental justice would most likely falter and all that he has done may not remain justified in context-to him.

This man is, however, far more dangerous than I am. I know that. Unfortunately, I know little about this man, his mentality, and the degree of his power.

All I know is that this man hates me to a paramount, and he fosters an incomprehensible amount of malice and contempt targeted towards me. I've encountered him directly thrice before, and I've fought a countless number of his pawns throughout my time in *the black and white.*

The life I lead is for reasons that I cannot explain to you right now. But I hope, deeply doctor, that you will have accumulated enough trust in me to realise that what I do...is for the good. The only good thing about this entire dynamic is that he knows as little of me-as I do of him. Therefore, if I can manoeuvre through my own mist, I can predict how he will manoeuvre through his.

That is all-that you need to know...for now."

Dr Shah remained stunned, unable to speak. His expressions were quizzical, and as he squinted his eyes, Dr Shah found himself in a deeply contemplative state.

The writer looked sympathetically at the doctor and said "don't worry that hard doctor. Get some rest, I'll see you in the...hmph..." The writer sighed as he paused for a fraction of a second, and then

said "later. I'll see you...later." With that the writer left the doctor
alone, for him to ponder upon all that was said in the last hour.

CHAPTER VI

The Exponential Stride

"I am sure that my newly made companion thinks me to be clinically insane; or maybe he believes that his own mind has wandered beyond the edge of sanity. Whatever it may be, he is fearful. That proves to be a massive disadvantage to my occupation, for he may resort to cowardice when I need him the most. My opening explanation, of the life I lead, had him speechless; I can only imagine what shall become of him when he finds himself trapped amid my endeavours. I have already told him, fellow reader, that his life is of lesser value to me than my occupation, for often when I contemplate, I come to the conclusion that my own life is of lesser value to me than my occupation.

This is the end. Hemant Shah will lead his life back into the grey. I will lead my life back into Hell...for now. But to do this I need to remain distant. Calculative. That's just my second nature. The doctor is going to expect strange atrocities for a few days, and then...he'll forget about it. He MUST forget about it. I need him to forget, so that I can bring him back stronger. He must also become a more prominent figure in his own life. He needs confidence. He needs substantial egocentrism-to make his life prominent enough in the grey so that he blurs out the memory of his time within the reaches of the black and the white. Psychogenic Amnesia. That's what the doctor needs. And of course, some Dellirictus should be perfect afterwards. To reel him back into it. To get him curious, once more. To get him to find me!"

A few days had passed since Hemant's last encounter with the so-called Quilton Addams; and Shah appeared to be in no hurry to meet him again. Strangely, after being involved in the eccentric's life for a few days, the doctor's life had taken a positive turn. He no longer sulked, rather he tried to cherish every singular moment. A sudden boost of confidence fuelled Dr Shah into work and his other endeavours, and an aura of dominance and tenacity remained, permanently fixated on the man. This sudden change in his attitude, intimidated most of his colleagues, as well as his senior doctors; and soon Hemant worked up the ranks to find himself in the medical practising position that he had always deserved. Dr Shah was now deliberate on clutching onto opportunities until he became a successor. No obstruction, now, could stop him from being at the end of a stream of constant achievements.

The day never came, however. Days turned to weeks and weeks turned to a month, as Dr Shah waited for the writer- who had said that he'd be back. However, the mad writer never again appeared in sight of Dr Shah, and soon enough...Dr Shah blocked the whole incident out of his memory; being able to recall nothing of the 2-day long trauma. His attitude towards life, however, never changed and his brilliant demeanour paired with his unmatched skill made him one of the most famous practitioners in London.

Dr Hemant Shah's work had become so popular, that he saw several important figures from time to time, whether it be a stomach-ache of the daughter of the wealthiest businessman, or full-on surgery on a member of the congress; Dr Shah was the man to be called. So famous had the man become, that his work extended beyond the rules of his medical practising position and oftentimes he was hired privately to conduct various different practices ranging in all elements from the medical spectrum. His efficiency and finesse always showed in his work, and soon his image and wealth took off on an exponential stride.

Life had suddenly become brilliant for Dr Shah, and that was all because of his encounter with the writer; but Dr Shah never recalled this experience. He had completely forgotten about the black and white and assumed his position on the hierarchy of the grey world.

A few months had passed. It was another Tuesday morning, and Dr Shah remained focused on the morning newspaper; while his breakfast-consisting of two pieces of perfectly cooked and crisp toasts, with one messy heap of brightly coloured scrambled eggs sandwiched in between, and a cup of black coffee-sat in front of him. As he ran his finger along the dainty text, that beautifully explained the current stock market situations, and what the politicians and sport stars had been up to, something caught his eye. It was surprising that he had not noticed it for so long, as it was the very headline of the newspaper. As Dr Hemant Shah commenced upon reading the bold letters of the newspaper, he involuntarily picked up his cup of coffee and began sipping through the warm and caffeinated liquid. The headline read:

"The streets of London seemed to get more and more violent! Recently, one of the stores of the Jewellery company owned by Alverez brothers, in the heart of the Northern portion of the city, was ambushed by a mysterious figure. The store-owning brothers, who rarely are present in the stores, had the misfortune of being present for management and business purposes that one night. They were found lying on the floor at dawn, and later put into immediate medical care. Thiago Alverez, the younger brother and the brand ambassador of the international company, was badly injured and found to have a dislocated shoulder as well as several bruise marks around his body. The entrepreneurial elder brother, Eduardo Alverez, was found to be in a stranger medical situation. Medical professionals have suggested that a mysterious air pocket was created in Mr Alverez's throat that prevented him from breathing for several moments. This caused him to collapse, however, being found soon after the ambush, he was attended to, and is said to be alive.

The head detective inspector of this case is none other than the eagle-eyed James Rex, who seems very excited about this case and extremely determined to find the mystery criminal. In our brief interview on the crime scene, he said:

"Our man is a professional. Judging the curious location of the bruise marks on the victims and efficacy with which the work was conducted in minutes, I can say that this man is slender in nature and is very acrobatic in fighting. He seems to have mastered several fighting techniques, and he definitely has expertise in this profession. Hence, he should have no direct or visible motive to ambush a random jewellery

store. This is not a single crime, but just one end of a thread that has seemed to create a massive web of criminal affairs. For this reason, we must investigate the jewellery company itself and every other company and brand it is connected to; as well as the elite individuals who are acquainted with the Alverez brothers."

On digging further, we've found some CCTV footage from a camera that has an overview of the unlucky store from the front. The footage shows the shadowy figure of the mystery ambusher slide across the camera after the ambush. Specifics of his face and other features are blurred; however, the silhouette seems to have carried a metallic bag and worn an expensive trench coat."

As Dr Shah read through the text, his hairs stood vertically over his skin, and a distinguished chill ran down his spine. He felt a strange connection to the news, as though he had already known who the mysterious man was. As Dr Shah reached the end of the text, his eyes widened, and his face turned to the colour of a ghastly pale shade. On reading the last sentence, he spit out the coffee, in sheer shock, and as the black liquid fountained across his living room, the image of the mad writer going by the alias of Quilton Addams established itself in Dr Hemant Shah's head!

CHAPTER VII

The Jewellery Shop Owners

"Shah...I don't really understand your sudden enthusiasm towards these patients." said the man, with dark grey hair, a grizzly moustache, tree bark-brown eyes and stout and round stature. He stared at Dr Hemant Shah with an air of confusion.

"I'm aware of how strange this seems; me suddenly becoming so keen about this case. Nothing to suspect, however. Sir, I am simply intrigued by it... I mean, seriously, a 'mysterious air-pocket'? You know my practising capabilities, and uh, I think my second opinion about this case could assist in curing these...uh, well...curious set of patients." Said Shah clumsily, however, with unwavering conviction.

"Hemant...We've known each other for a while. You an' I have seen a lot of cases. You should know best that in these cases a lot is confidential...it's a bomb of sorts. Any wrong move and the hospital's name could be dragged into the mud. Plus...we already don't know what we've got ourselves into. No one...can really identify...what actually happened to Mr Alverez and his brother, after they were admitted. We've barely done anything, man. I mean, just yesterday, the assigned doctors came to me and said that...uh...oh God, what is this mess, Shah? What have we gotten ourselves into? Well, it seems that somehow, those wounds and the infamous 'mysterious air-pocket'...somehow, they have naturally healed...and I mean...healed by themselves! It's crazy!

The police forensics department has been harassing our doctors and begging for answers because they are baffled, and all the doctors on the case are working through the mist- completely on vague hints and medical intuition. And if that were not, our fellow patients seem extremely...shady. They have these massive bodyguards staying in their room 24/7, and they keep making our doctors uncomfortable. In addition, to that the patients themselves have been so ambiguous about the event, as though they are hiding something. What if... they really are hiding something? All this is just so weird. The damn CONFUSION! It's getting to me! It's so blimmin' hard to speculate and identify the problem when the patient is not willing to give you the details."

"Then you should be happy that I'm willing to volunteer. I mean the greater the number of hands on this case, the faster the work shall be done. Come on! This is your opportunity to make things easier..."

"Yes, but I have the responsibility of handling all the hands on this case and it already seems way to complicated. Personally, Hemant, I don't want you to get entangled in this affair. It'd be better if you cared a little more about the brilliant reputation that you've built. Plus...you appearing out of nowhere might freak out the patients... they already seem selective about whom they give information to. If you just pop up into their wardroom...we might, well, we might end up losing our clients. And-and losing them...might just be a good thing...but I can't just let you barge in on a case like th..."

"C'mon Halls. Just give this one to me. I can feel it! I can help you out. I can DO this..."

"But they're already bloody healed, Shah! What else can you possibly do? We are just left in the mud with two suspicious patients whom we can't let go- oh no, we can't- 'cause the bleeding cops want answers! Yeah-yeah, the people who are supposed to be finding the answers THEMSELVES, want *us* to solve their problem! So...tell me Dr Hemant Shah-what on this god's earth will YOU do?" Dr Hall's frustration finally explicitly manifested itself into speech. His anger, his fear, his distress all mingled together to form a singular unit of irritation. He continued to manically look Hemant up and down-expecting an answer. However, Dr Shah remained unfazed. He subverted his gaze for a moment, looking up to the white-tiled ceiling, and then with the plainest of expressions, Shah stared back at Dr Halls.

"Sir...I will do...something. I will interrogate them!"

Dr Benedict Halls stared at the walls for a moment. The sudden uproar of enthusiasm in Hemant had pushed Dr Halls into silence. He had to think. His eyes remained fixated upon the epicentre of his vision. He remained in a state of deep contemplation, as his eye-brows rose and sunk while sweat droplets precipitated out of his forehead. His pale skin looked paler as the artificial and monochromatic light, from his office tube-light, illuminated it, and his fingers quivered. He sat silently for a while, and Dr Shah continued to eye him down…with an air of irritation mixed with wistfulness. Finally, Dr Halls looked back at Hemant.

"Interrogate them? You?" asked Dr Benedict Halls, as he briskly thwarted his train of thoughts. Hemant Shah-a man who could barely talk to the hospital receptionist; who could barely keep his personal information from revealing itself by hanging out of his shirt pocket; who did not seem to contain within him an ounce of confidence.

However now, he was Hemant Shah- a man who changed his whole demeanour in the span of two days; who now brimmed with tenacity and social prowess; who demanded for a 200% increase in salary to the owner of the hospital, with his chest out; who remained fearless in front of his medical rivals. Hemant Shah- the medical powerhouse; the one-man-hospital; the king of surgeries.

"Yes. Interrogate them. ME."

"Hmph…" Sighed Dr Benedict Halls, "Fine. if you want to do this so badly-for whatever godforsaken reason-you shall."

It worked. Dr Hemant Shah was in the clear, and he was GOING to find some ANSWERS!

If Detective Inspector James Rex was as sharp as they say, then the Alverez brothers were the answer to all his questions…and maybe they were the key to understanding what was happening.

As Hemant silently contemplated, he realised he was drawn to this mystery for no apparent reason. He had no motive and no purpose to participate, yet he was extremely desperate to get to the bottom of this 'jewellery ambush' affair. Something strange slowly crept up Hemant's spine. Something new. Was it excitement? Was it the thrill of it all? Hemant could not tell, but he knew that he loved 'Something'!

"The Dellirictus is working. In this induced state of delirium his emotions shall only be controlled by curiosity and adrenaline. And, of course, I'll be there to look over his shoulders-making sure he doesn't mess up. The doctor's enthusiasm has awoken once more. He'll no longer fear our twisted reality. I need him to get to the bottom of this. I need HIM to thwart The Stygian's plans."

"Find anything? "A man questioned. He had pitch-black eyes that could glare at one's soul and entice one at the same time. His ebony skin shined at the edges as they reflected the patch of light. The man wore a grey trench coat, under which he had donned classic formals- a black tie-on top of his white shirt, tucked into his grey trousers. His shoes were made out of leather; however, their soles were rubbery and sturdy... perfect for running. He smiled, as sunlight hit his face, and his smoothly barbered, militarised buzz haircut, as well as his perfectly groomed beard glinted.

"Not really detective...sir." The lady in blue replied." We've looked everywhere. There seems to be nothing that was stolen. I mean obviously there wasn't much to steal...was there...ha-ha...sarcasm! Sorry. Um... besides the signs of struggle around the cashier table and one of the glass-encased showpiece mantles smashed, we couldn't find anything."

"Well, that's rather disappointing, Martha...and I expected so much from you." The man in the trench coat sighed.

"Y-you...know m-my name?" Asked the uniformed officer.

"Oh yes." Said the man with an air of confidence," You've inspected several break-ins and robberies...have you not? This should be your forte, Officer Bennet."

"Yes sir...but I guess my skill is limited. No promotion still, you see? Yay...ha-ha; sorry again."

"Well Martha, it's no promotion...yet. You never know..."

"Well...we did find something else, actually, but we didn't think much of it." Said Martha.

"And whatever may that be?" asked the man...with a slightly mocking tone.

"It's this coin." Said the uniformed officer as she showed the specimen to her superior. "It seems to be counterfeit...except it doesn't resemble any currency on the planet. It's got this intricate design...and a bold, capital B as its logo. Us uniformed folks just assumed it was of little importance."

"Let me have a closer look, would ya?" the man said as he took the specimen "Hmm...the plot thickens!"

"What can you make of it sir?"

"Martha...you may end up getting that promotion after all...because...you've just hit the jackpot! I mean...obviously you still have to give the test for the position of detective, but...this, well this is...some clean work." The man said with dormant excitement. As the man continued to observe the coin, and as the officer continued to observe the man...a distinguished sound was heard. Soon enough, the man retired from his examination and shoved his hand in his coat pocket, to fetch his phone.

"You've reached Detective Inspector James Rex," the man said as he pressed his phone against his ear" what is the matter?"

"James...we've got it!" the voice on the other end began," if you don't get 'em now, Sharky... I still can't believe it. That warrant is a golden ticket!"

"Finally! If You were here, man, I'd give you a kiss!" The detective stopped...as he realised that the uniformed officer in front of him had flushed to a shade of scarlet.

"Oh...it's an exaggeration, officer...don't you worry."

"Oh no; I mean that's good...but...um... not that it's any of my concern...ha-ha...I...don't...sorry" fumbled Martha. Her superior laughed and continued to speak on the phone.

"Thank you...thank you...THANK YOU! Oh man, how did you get the permit and..." The detective stopped himself again," Uhm...Martha...do you have anything else to add?"

"Uh...what? Oh! No...I'm...I don't think...I, well, I..."

"You can go dear."

"Thank you...sorry." The uniformed officer said, before she walked quickly to the far end of the other side of the crime scene.

CHAPTER VIII

The Spirit Of Quilton Addams

"The night is dark-shadows continue to dance at the edges of the landscape, as though trying to correspond to the twinkling of stars across the horizon.

I need to make sense out of chaos.

The plan worked in my favour. Dr Shah had assumed his esteemed position in the hierarchy of the grey. He gained all that there was to be gained. And now...he's back. His curiosity will help me. I'm sure of it. In addition, fellow reader, he needs to be helping ME. He needs to be on...my side. For if he's not, then they'll get to him. They'll use him and then discard him. That's why I'm disgusted by them. That's why I must end them.

It was a perfect ambush. It really was clean work. I left no clues...except for the fake ones that I planted. However, the grey world was quick to draw attention to the case...I am sure Shah has found his enthusiasm for the black and white rekindling. I had dozed him with enough cholinergic to spike this rekindling. Only time will tell if the drugs do their job. For now, it looks like I need to meet an old friend."

The night sky twinkled with stars as though Uranus had chosen to wear a gown embedded with the most expensive diamonds. Underneath the natural twinkling, several artificial street lamps flickered and LEDs from several billboards and posters illuminated central London. The sign that usually read 'Pellington Hospital', at the top of the five-storey building, had a few letters that refused to glow against the starry night and therefore now the sign could only read 'P---i-g--- --spit—'. Facing the hospital with the unfortunately mocking sign, Brooke's pub remained...with vibrant light and sweet, melodious music coming out of the dingy yet sophisticated structure.

Inside, Dr halls sat at the bar, with two mammoth jugs of golden-brown liquid and spoke stutteringly. "I still don't get how those fools ended up getting mugged by some two-bit thug, even though they walk around with so many damned bodyguards!"

"You know Dr Halls," Shah said, as he approached the bar to bid A Dieu to his senior colleague before the interrogation "he was no regular burglar."

Being reminded of Mr Quilton Addams, Shah found himself in a certain trans- an emotional vortex of sorts. He could not describe what he was feeling, but they were strong and impactful emotions-confusing and bemusing. He never understood why, but the thought of Quilton Addams brought those emotions to life. It was as though someone had hit Hemant in the head with a metal bat and he had started bleeding; however, blood was still surging through his brain...like he was some magical bottomless blood bag with an unfortunate dent. As in, he constantly received blood and constantly lost blood...and in that state of constant surge and loss of oxygen to his brain, Hemant imagined that someone tried to drown him, but somehow, he could breathe under the water he was being drowned in. That seemed to be the only way Hemant could describe what it felt like when he thought of the man named Quilton Addams--just an array of conflicting emotions.

"Burglar or not- I can't care." Retorted back Dr Halls-in a partially drunken state.

"Thank you for clearing out the bodyguards...sir." Said Hemant and he swiftly walked out of the pub and into the Hospital from across the street.

"What? I haven't done that."

"Well, you have now, Halls. Thanks again." Replied Hemant as he turned and started approaching the pub's exit.

"Don't do anything stupid!" yelled Dr Benedict halls drunkenly without looking at the door through which Shah had walked out.

Why did Hemant care about this ambush? He did not know; Why was he drawn to this case? He did not know; Why did he want to unravel the mystery of the man named Quilton Addams? He did not know. Only one thing, and one thing alone was perfectly clear to Shah- he was once again treading through the black and white fogs-and Hemant loved every bit of it!

The bars of LED flickered randomly as Hemant walked through the hospital corridor. The nut-brown room doors appeared to be darker due to the flickering illuminations, and the plain white tiles of the floor glistened...even during the short intervals of complete darkness. The entire area was exhaustively practising a daunting atmosphere, as though it was a manifestation of one of the several chambers of hell. Hemant gulped, and his walking pace increased rapidly.

Nevertheless, he found himself in the brightly lit reception soon enough, and in front of him sat the sweet and lovely receptionist- Kim Nguyen. Hemant's heart rate slowed down instantaneously, and he smiled at the ever-friendly face of the receptionist.

"Are the Alverez brot..." Hemant began, but Kim seemingly read his mind.

"Yeah, Doc. The bodyguards have cleared out, so you don't need to worry 'bout that. You can go to them now." Said Kim with a very calm and pleasant tone.

"Ok! Uh...I mean...thank you, thank you...Kim" said Hemant as he approached the other side of the hospital. As Hemant got closer and closer to room 606, the lights began to flicker more and more. Out in the distance, through one of the corridor windows, Hemant saw a massive streak of lighting strike the terrains and soon enough thunder cracked loud and deep. The atmosphere had gone back to its former demeanour, and by the looks of it, was not keen on becoming calm and dainty anytime soon.

"Now...or never." Hemant said to himself, as he sprang himself at the doors of room 606 and clutched on the door knob. Hemant snatched the door out from its hinges and thunder cracked as his darkened silhouette entered the room swiftly.

There was a momentary pause in the cabin. Nature had halted upon its actions. The herculean and violent storm had turned to light drizzling. Nothing-no external factor remained to hold tension in the room. All that the brothers saw was the dark silhouette, light reflecting off of the rectangular spectacles that it wore. The brothers felt Dr Shah's presence-felt it in their blood deficient veins. A cold shudder ran through the entirety of the cabin.

"Que? Qué deseas? What do you want?" Began one of the Alverez, desperate to murder the unsettling tension, "What do you...", but thunder cracked again and abruptly interrupted the patient's speech. Nature was on Hemant's side. The atmosphere was on Hemant's side. He was the only one who was to speak. The dark silhouette of the doctor glistened at the edges as another streak of lightning zapped the terrains of earth from the heavens. His eyes gleamed in sophisticated contemplation.

At that very moment, Dr Shah was not mortal. He was not a man with singular talent or interest. He was not himself. At that very moment, Hemant Shah had become a concept, an ideology, a symbol. At that very moment...Hemant Shah had become QUILTON ADDAMS.

The corresponding thunder broke the ominous silence, opening the stage as the dark silhouette began. "The Alverez brothers...hmph" Dr Shah sighed, as he continued in a whispery voice, "tell me, who attacked you?"

"Are you with the police?" Thiago Alverez asked, while he gently lifted his bruised neck over his chest, just enough to carefully analyse the silhouette from a laying position. "We've told them everything." Said the laying man...his voice growing deeper, as he recovered from the prior tension in the room.

"I...ask the questions...here." Said Shah with an air of stoic dominance, "And you...will tell me whatever I desire to know."

"El Tonto! I already told you. WE'VE ALREADY TOLD THE POL..."

"Détente! Thiago...pay some respect to our...guest." Spoke the elder brother. Hemant could tell he was superior. Eduardo Alverez held an honoured position in the conversation. He was far more intellectual and decisive than his short-tempered brother. "Ask me, stranger...whatever it is that you want to ask."

"My question remains...unchanged. Who...attacked you?" asked Dr Shah in the same whispery and ominous voice.

"Have you read the news, Hermano? It was a mysterious man-- leather coat and all. He attacked us very swiftly...for no apparent reason. If you would have read the news you would..."

"Quit lying...Alverez." Interrupted Dr Shah, "Deception...won't get you out of this one. Your expressions are too emotive...to conceal your inner thoughts. Well, you're thinking is right. I am dangerous, and I will...hurt you, if you do not speak the truth. I know the man who attacked you had a motive. You will tell me what this motive was. Now!"

Silence filled the room once again. Thiago Alverez stared at Hemant thickly, while his elder brother viciously glanced across the room. Eduardo Alverez's eyes danced violently as he thought.

"He was pretty young." Thiago broke the silence. "A man of about 25 years. He was swift. Acrobatic. He wanted something that we entirely do not..."

"Possess." Spat out Eduardo Alverez, "This man sought something that we do not entirely possess. Something that is much greater than our company...our beloved Pequeno Diamante."

"What?" Spoke Dr Shah.

"We don't know." Replied the brothers in unison.

The dark silhouette slowly moved across the room. Back and forth. The brothers remained lying down-waiting for a reaction of some sort. However, the silhouette managed to remain emotively lifeless. All it did was move-in a uniformed manner. Whether the stranger was contemplating or relieving stress or thinking, the Alverez brothers did not know.

"Since the two of you haven't understood what I've said," The silhouette of Dr Hemant Shah began, "allow me to demonstrate. I said...I will hurt you." Said the silhouette and as it did so, it gently moved towards Thiago Alverez and twisted the pinky toe on his left foot malevolently.

"AHHHHRGG!" Screamed the younger brother in pain. His eyes teared up as the sudden pain took over his entire body and mind.

"Fifth Metatarsal Fracture." Said the silhouette in the ominous and whispery voice," Don't worry you'll walk…if you tell me-everything. If not…then I've four other toe fingers to break. Then, Immobilization would be…imminent."

"You're sick!" Declared Eduardo Alverez as he looked at his brother worriedly. "You're crazy!"

"Well…pain…is the best teacher." Said the silhouette as he approached the fourth toe finger on Thiago Alverez's left foot.

"Arrggh…JUST TELL HIM, damm!" cursed Thiago Alverez.

"Hell's Kitchen…New York! That's where you'll find the damn motive!" Exclaimed Eduardo Alverez.

"Why can't you tell me?" Asked the silhouette.

"We would get slaughtered." Said Ontario Alverez with dreaded earnestness.

"Why?" Demanded Shah.

"Slaughtered." Eduardo Alverez repeated softly.

"WHY!" Shouted the daunting silhouette. However, no response came. The Alverez brothers were not going to speak further. Apparently, whatever the motive was- it was something to do with someone…someone who possessed far more dominion over the Alverez brothers-perhaps even more than Quilton Addams himself.

Whatever resided in the undergrounds of Hell's Kitchen…surely was not pleasant. Criminal? Most likely!

Dr Shah sighed and his silhouette left the darkness of cabin 606.

CHAPTER IX

A Man Of Law

The jagged bars of luminosity across the horizon of the hospital corridors continued to flicker indifferently. The atmosphere had once again lost its respect for Hemant Shah just as he had lost the essence of Quilton Addams. Back to his regular demeanour, Shah felt his heart pounding against the gates of his skeletal rib-cage. His eyes remained unblinking, pointlessly following the reflections of the blinding monochromatic light that spilled out of the LED bars at the ceiling. It was hard to concentrate again, and Dr Hemant Shah no longer possessed the natural tranquillity that he had allowed himself a few moments ago in cabin 606. It was as though a spirit of sheer power and superiority had exited Hemant's bodily vessel, leaving behind a husk of a man-incapable and shrivelled. He needed to become the silhouette...he needed to become Quilton Addams...once again.

But how? What was Dr Hemant Shah's purpose in the realm that separated the dark from light? As he stood at the centre of the corridor, he questioned himself. Why was he so eager to dive back into the sea of the black and white? Why did he feel the need to interfere? His life had taken a brilliant turn. He had the money, the fame, and the admiration. What was it then that drove him back to the edge of the grey world?

Hemant kept asking himself, interrogating his own conscience in a hurried frenzy; but alas, nothing of significance could be uncovered. Hemant could not come close to identifying the cause of his urge. Yet, he knew what he wanted to do. Hell's Kitchen. That is where he needed to be. That is where trouble was. That is where Quilton Addams would be. That is where the answers lurked. And Hemant...he needed ANSWERS!

"Oi, you alright, mate?" A gruff and concerned voice with a thick accent, broke the silence and pulled Hemant back into the present.

"Huh? Oh yeah...I'm alright, thanks." Hemant managed as he looked up to see who he was talking to. The man in front of him gave Hemant a professional smile-impersonal yet assuring. He had a neatly done Buzz cut and a perfectly groomed beard, along with pitch black eyes that could stare into one's soul and entice them simultaneously. His attire shined as the hospital lights targeted their artificial rays at the clothing: An expensive coat, striped shirt, trousers, and custom leathered shoes.

"How are the infamous brothers doing then, doctor?" asked the man

"Well, they're...difficult." Hemant managed. He still could not figure out who the man was, yet he knew he had seen the man somewhere. "Why, are you one of their clients? Or maybe someone close?"

"Nah mate. I'm the guy who's 'bout to bash their heads in, if they don't give me some bloody answers!" Said the man with a prideful vigour.

"James Rex!" Hemant blurted out. The hammer of realisation had finally struck Hemant's nail-head, and he continued to stare at the detective with awe.

"In the bloody flesh." The detective began "say, it's time for me to have a little chat with your patients. Is that alright?"

Hemant smiled at the mocking tone that the man spoke with. It reminded him of another individual who constantly mocked him for a span of two days and then disappeared entirely.

"Do your worst, officer." He said before slowly walking away.

"Good man." The detective spoke for one last time and then swiftly entered cabin 606.

The pain could not have been worse for Thiago Alverez. He continuously shuffled under the rusty woollen blanket of his hospital bed with dormant agony that treaded back and forth along the bony lines of his left foot. On the far end of the other side, Eduardo Alverez pondered the identity of the mystery silhouette. His face contorted to showcase and excruciatingly rigid expression that appeared even more mangled due to the shadows that hid in the cracks and creases of his face. The darkness was the doing. It gave Eduardo Alverez a menacing look-the look of a man plotting and planning. Was the mystery silhouette the ambusher? But the questions...the silhouette asked questions with answers that were already known to the ambusher. Who was this man? Was he just another inquisitive doctor? But doctors don't randomly break toes, not even the psychopathic ones. Who was he then? Perhaps a member of... "No, it can't be." Mr Alverez thought to himself.

"Y-you t-think....argh...t-that it was...hmph...an inside man?" Croaked Thiago Alverez through the pain. His pupils fluttered raucously within the prisons of his own eyes-desperate for relief.

"It...can't be." Mr Eduardo Alverez replied as he temporarily tore out of his state of deep contemplation, before diving back in to the depths of his own mind. Was it possible? Was the mysterious silhouette just a pressure device, something to keep the Jewellery owning brothers on their toes? Could it really have been an elaborate, covert measure to test their...loyalty? No. The questions. The questions were an explicit hint pointing towards the identity of the mysterious silhouette. This man was no insider, not some mere agent of The Stygian. This man...was a Rogue.

"So...Mr Alverez and...Mr Alverez," a gruff voice spoke as the door to the cabin opened from the outside "what...happened?" The brothers uncomfortably raised their heads above their torso from their perpetual lying position to get a better glimpse of the source of the voice. It was a man, one with an athletic and muscular build. His head remained tilted downwards, which told the brothers that the man kept his undivided focus on them; his facial expressions and clothes, however, remained as elements of ambiguity. All the light from the corridors outside seemed to hit the brothers, illuminating them perfectly, avoiding the man at the door. He remained unlit. He remained daunting.

"You...y-you again!" grumbled Thiago Alverez, shuffling in his single-bed, as a sudden rage began to mix with his physical pain.

"I w-will...hmph...I-I will Kill y-you! Break as many t-toes...as y-you want. I'll still s-stand; and then...y-you'll d-die!" Exclaimed

Thiago as he felt his temper slowly rise again. YOU PIECE OF…"

"DÉTENTE!" Eduardo Alverez's voice pierced through his brother's and terminated it altogether. "He is different. Calm down, hermano. He's with the law. Isn't that right, officer?"

"That's…Detective Inspector to you…Mr Alverez." The man at the door spoke with a formal yet comfortingly gentle tone. "Now, it seems as though I've missed a good chunk of the story, eh? So, tell me Thiago…"

"You may speak to me, officer." Eduardo Alverez hastily interrupted the man at the door. "My brother is in a lot of pain, and…"

"Listen," The voice from the door became deathly soft. It no longer remained gentle and accommodating "let us lads make one thing very…very clear. It is I who will do…the talking. You…will simply respond. So, keep your answers short…and sweet; and never…INTERUPT ME!" Thiago Alverez straightened up cautiously on his bed, while his elder brother remained quiet. Mr Eduardo Alverez was very good at reading the room. Just a moment ago he had deduced the man at the door to be a police officer. However, Ontario Alverez no longer could sense the gentle officer at the door. Now, all that he felt was the demanding hands of law pointing their sword-like fingers at him. Thiago Alverez gulped.

"As I was saying, Thiago, why are you angry?" The man from the door spoke. Eduardo Alverez violently darted his eyes at his brother, desperately trying to caution him; but it simply had no effect. His brother looked at the dark humanoid shape at the door thickly, for a few seconds. His pain had suddenly turned dormant. All that was active in the violently pumping heart of Thiago Alverez…was fear.

"Someone…Officer…I-well, someone came in earlier and… a-and b-broke…my…pinky toe." Murmured Thiago Alverez.

The officer seemed unaffected by the mention of this strange act and continued to question the patients calmly "And…you wanted to kill them for this reason?"

"Naturally."

"Right. I'm sure you just said it in the heat of the moment. Surely, you don't actually kill people?"

"Officer, of course n-not. Yes, I was j-just angry, and I..."

"Or...get people killed?" The officer interrupted dominantly.

"Uh...ha...o-of course not...officer."

"Nothing funny here, Thiago." The man at the door spoke "A lot of people get others...killed. People with money, people with power, people with connections. Perhaps...people who own a multi-millionaire jewellery company. All one needs...is a contract. And of course, Mr Alverez, a connection...to the darker side makes it easier."

"Officer, these are not questions!" Eduardo spoke enraged. "You will not make my brother uncomfortable in this manner, badge or no badge."

"Sir, all that you need to do is cooperate..."

"We were attacked in our own cabin, in a bloody hospital! Do you realize how incompetent you and your worthless task force will look when the news gets out? That you couldn't even protect the people in your damned protective custody!" howled Eduardo Alverez regaining a sense of psychological victory over the man at the door.

"IF...the news gets out; Mr Alverez. You're right. IF the news gets out...my crew will look bad. This case might even get reassigned to another detective. Well...perhaps..." the man swiftly took out his pistol and pointed it at the patients "perhaps, I should just kill you myself."

"You can't...you cannot do this you police scum. You'll die for this!" screamed Eduardo Alverez, losing all his calm and mental diplomacy, manically howling in rage and fear like an animal.

"Shut up! You cannot possibly comprehend how easy this is for me, Mr Alverez. My position in the force allows me...loopholes. I have done this countless times, Mr Alverez! However, if you cooperate...I will act accordingly."

"The man who left just as you entered broke my toe. It hurt like crazy. He questioned us about the ambusher. He questioned us about his motive. And we told him that..." blurted out Thiago Alverez in hopes to calm the man at the door, but his voice was shot down by the man.

"You told him that whatever the ambusher wanted was something that you did not entirely possess. Then this man asked you the reason for this, and you told him that you would get slaughtered if you told him." The officer finished Thiago's sentence.

"Exactly so!" the brothers exclaimed in unison.

"Penfeather! It was him. He was the ambusher. He was the mystery man in your cabin. He came back to trick you into giving him more information. Oh lord, this is rich! That bastard fooled me into thinking that he was a doctor. It all makes sense. The way he was in the hallway, the way he said 'do your worst'-that's his signature line! Oh man...Penfeather, how many disguises can you afford, you..."

"Who?" The brothers asked, absolutely oblivious.

"The coin that you had...you were supposed to bring it to the ceremony, were you not? But you idiots lost it! It is almost time, and still you fools did not even think that a rogue could have been planning to rob you of the two most important artefacts belonging to The Stygian-the coin and the box. He has the coin now! He's close to discovering everything now! Centuries worth of legacy ruined because of you two!"

"What...coin?" asked the brothers.

"Don't play dumb with me. The coin with the giant capital B at its epicentre. The prototype! I'm sure the monarchs of The Stygian would be very disappointed if they found out that the gatekeepers of their lair fumbled the one job that they had."

"YOU KNOW!" The brothers spoke in sheer excitement. "But...how?"

"Listen, the man you've just met is a rogue. He knows about the coin...he knows about The Stygian. He knows how the coin works. How it fits into the box. The one thing that he doesn't know is the whereabouts of the door. Right?" The man at the door came closer and bent down towards the patients so that they could see him better. The brothers guiltily stared at the officer's perfectly groomed beard.

"Oh no. I know that look. Please tell me...please tell me, for the love of God, that you did not tell this man about Hell's Kitchen." The brothers did not speak, but only glanced back and forth, and at each other.

"Listen, officer...we were in an inferior position. He could have hurt us real bad!" Eduardo Alverez finally broke the silence. "But...but n-now that we know that all of us work for the High Order, we can...we can figure something out! We can find and kill this man, right? Get rid of him entirely, senor. Right? You can trust us now, and we can trust you. From one Tartarean to another."

"IDIOTS! You can't possibly kill a rogue, especially not this one. You've ruined months of planning! Hmph..." The officer sighed and calmed himself down. "You remember Mr Alverez, when I said that I would act accordingly if you and your brother cooperated?" Asked the detective inspector airily.

"Y-yes...we do" The brothers replied in unison, slowly glancing back at each other, as a sense of triumph flooded their eyes.

"I lied." Said the man as he pulled out his gun.

"NO NO NO!" screamed the brothers. But it was too late. It ended as soon as it had begun. Two shots-clean and quick. The momentous screams metamorphosed back swiftly into natural silence, and the man named James Rex stood in it. He stood in the silence-remorseless and static. However, his mind zoomed the neural paths-stimuli after stimuli being shot into the sea of grey matter in his brain, as he thought at a vigorously rapid speed. It was time. Time for damage control; and Detective Inspector James Rex wasted none of it.

CHAPTER X

Kim Nguyen

"The air around the hospital seems...sombre. The sulphurous stench of wrong-doing is evident; I can smell it from here. On the rooftop of a neighbouring building, I sit...waiting-waiting for the right moment. It has been an hour since my acquaintance went into the hospital, and I need to discuss urgent matters with him. The Pellington hospital has succumbed to an air of malignance, and as the night unfolds further, the stench of sulphur just becomes more and more...prominent. That is the fashionable attribute of agents of Tartaroux. Vile creatures they are. Human...technically yes, but professionally they are-demons. Devils with an unmatched lust for horror and pain. A rogue works against them. But it isn't hard, fellow reader, to sympathise with a Tartarean. They, unfortunately, almost always have pasts that justify their diabolic actions of the present. But rogues have similar pasts; life breaks us differently. A worker of The Stygian chooses to fight the fire of life with the enraged fire within, whereas we choose to harness the warmth of this lively fire. It is acceptance truly that makes us different breeds. A Tartarean will never be able to accept that life has the upper hand. Rogues, on the contrary, operate within the spontaneity of life-accepting it as the superior power.

Wait. Something has changed. Oh no...Sharky...what have you done?

It is about to rain. I quiet like the rain. It makes...encounters...much more...interesting. I am an addict of climax. Desire for action is the only emotion I engage in, when not in the midst of pure instinctual logic. My work requires individuals of my metal. Those who desire conflict. Those who are fond of atrocities.

Is this all a metaphor? Am I just insane? Partially. But the truth is seeded into lies; and the insane are those who have the beautiful

44

ability to stand on the very line between truth and lies. But few know how to tread on this line. Few know how to use their position on this line as an advantage. Fellow reader, all my adventures have taught me the same value again and again: insanity pairs well with logic, not emotion. Those who get emotional-those who are not able to control their innate feelings, fall terribly on this line, and tip to either side. Some have lives that showcase the gruesome truth and nothing else, while some have lives made entirely out of hollow lies.

My acquaintance is the former archetype. He is righteous. Blinded by his own admiration for judicial justice. He is a man of law, and that is his biggest disadvantage. As I write this down, I see my acquaintance exit the hospital. He has two body bags with him. Whom is he carrying? The Alverez Brothers! Did he really end the Jewellery company owners? He couldn't have left the hospital without eyes turning towards him. He must have used his power. This man has immense power.

Interjection, fellow reader. We first need to fix those in the grey, who have unwantedly tasted the exhilaration of the black and white. The encounter can wait."

The dainty lights along the fine establishment of Brooke's Pub flickered against the darkness of the night sky. Looking up it was almost as though the sky was a canvas, which had been suddenly splashed with a handsome amount of darkened pigment by a clumsy painter. The stars sparkled like jewels embedded in a traditional designer gown or an expensive Indian sari-glistening in thematic coordination to their artificial counterparts around the pub and the rest of London. But jewels did not matter at the moment. Jewellery owners did. To be precise the actions committed to take hold of these jewellery owners mattered; and to be even more precise-the casualties of these actions mattered the most.

On a distant roof top of an abandoned construction site, a distinguished figure sat extremely still. The back of his trench coat fluttered vigorously in the air-the air that warned the dwellers of London of a nasty gale. The storm clouds were ever closer. The figure promptly closed his laptop and carefully put it inside his submetallic bag, which dangled along the left side of his torso. His clothes appeared as shabby as the silhouettes of the villainous storm clouds, and his thin, string-like belt, instead of being worn in regular fashion, remained tied across his waist like a rope-the metallic end dangling like the hand bag. He stared into the abyss of the night in London for a jarring minute. As still as a statue. It suddenly began to rain. The drizzling procured jittery oscillations along whatever surface the rain droplets came in contact with.

Suddenly the still figure jumped off the roof.

It would have been the strangest sight if any mortal soul would have cared to look. But no one looks towards an abandoned construction site in the middle of the night; especially not when it is raining. The construction site was roughly three storeys tall. Yet, the man seemed to have no preliminary thought. Just staring into the darkness and then...jump.

As the man fell, he pierced through vertical curtains of precipitation. His silhouette had contorted in dart-like fashion, where his hands were raised upwards, while his trench coat zipped past him to spread out vertically behind him, forming a daunting wing-like structure in raucous motion; and his feet were pointed sharply with utmost precision towards the ground, which came closer and closer. However, the man remained calm, whilst in his dynamic and acrobatic posture. It was almost as though he was waiting, even in the state of freefall, for the perfect moment; and the perfect moment came with brilliant punctuality. Right at the mouth of the last storey, with a nine-metre gap between the man and the gravel at the floor of the site, the man's rope-like belt flung out from his waist like a vicious, predatory snake, and wrapped its metallic end around a jagged steel bar, protruding out of a random portion of a wall. Right in time, right before the entirety of the reptilian belt flew out of reach, the man grabbed the other end, clinging onto it for stability. The nine-metre gap did not shorten in length any further. The free fall had been thwarted. The man was now securely dangling off the singular steel bar, his trench coat still fluttering in the midst of rain. The dangling individual gently pulled at his make-shift belt, which in turn pulled at the steel bar; and being a singular steel bar with decent ductility and flexibility, the steel bar complied and bended slowly-until the man was at a distance from the ground, where it was safe to let go. With a dynamic shrug that began at the man's feet and ended at the man's wrists, the man managed to whip his belt outwards until it unravelled and loosened its grip on the metal bar, before letting go altogether. With a quiet thud, the man had landed safely on the ground without a single injury, despite jumping from the height of 27 metres. The success of his activity failed to faze the man, however, and he continued to walk towards the light-towards Pellington hospital.

The storm unforgivingly unleashed its wrath onto the streets of London, forcing the people to seek shelter amid shops and pubs. A few ran back into their apartments, which were situated at the heart of the northern region of the city. But most people remained trapped in places they were meant to leave hours ago.

Kim Nguyen, the receptionist at Pellington hospital, sat at her desk leaning against the transparent, glass surface of her table. Her ocean-blue eyes contained a dazed expression, behind her elliptically framed spectacles. The corridor lights continued to flicker indifferently, illuminating the woollen turtle-neck in shades of orange, along with black jeans on Kim. She continued to stare outside the hospital, staring at the eternal droplets of water, which violently broke into smaller molecules as they came in vigorous contact with the concrete floors of the streets. Kim's natural friendliness and her receptionist's alertness had somehow abandoned her demeanour. She seemed to be in a strange trans. Her mind was preoccupied and blank simultaneously, and she seemed to notice nothing and care not at all about her surroundings. She just cared about the rain. She cared about the time, when it would stop. She cared about leaving; from where? Why? How? She could not possibly tell. But she wanted to leave. She wanted to be as far away as she could be from her current surroundings. However, it was not fear or frenzy that drove her to this state. No, it was a sense of exhilaration. A stimulus that had overdriven the satisfactory receptors of her brain, making her want to give up everything out of...happiness. In the midst of the trans, Kim felt as though her life's purpose was fulfilled in brilliant fashion, and her life now meant nothing. It was almost as though someone had put her under a spell that made her so happy-so ecstatic-that she wanted to end her own life. But that would not be possible in the rain. The rain needed to stop. So, Kim Nguyen waited with an emotion of patient impatience.

"As I walk closer and closer to the hospital, the scene becomes clearer. He has done a clean job, no loose ends. Except one it seems. She's dazed. I need to talk to her. I need to neutralise the Blursion. But that won't stop me from recording the moment, fellow reader. I am an expert in writing in the moment, and that is my favourite method to record my tales. So, let's begin, shall we?"

As Kim Nguyen stared at the translucent front gates from inside the hospital, from her desk, a silhouette began to grow more and more prominent. Just a tiny black smear at first-like a dot amid the general grey gradient of the condensed rain droplets on the door. However, gradually, the dot turned into a speck; the speck turned into a smear; and the smear soon enough turned into a puddle of black shadows formulating at the epicentre of the twin gates-spliced by the metal locks that ran down the middle of the two doors. Kim's trans was interrupted. Kim did not like that. Suddenly the door flung open from the outside.

"The element of surprise is most important. I needed to catch her off guard. I need to reduce the intensity of the Blursion. I need to pull her out from her own mind. She needs to stop thinking to counter the sedative. And that won't be too hard because she will have her focus subverted- BY ME."

The man on the other side of the open doors stared directly at the receptionist.

"H-how may I help...y-you...sir?" The receptionist mumbled uncontrollably. Kim suddenly realised that it was impossible for her to speak without stuttering. The man at the door had a face devoid of expression. He just stared at her, with one of his hands folded behind him-holding a phone on which he appeared to be typing. However, it was not clear if he was. He could have very well been holding something else behind his back, or may be nothing at all. But one feature that was as clear as crystals, to Kim, was that the man held his left hand deliberately behind his back.

"S-Sir, what it is...erm.... what....is it... that y-you need?" Kim tried to speak again. There was a brief pause. The man's face remained expressionless. Kim momentarily forgot about the rain. Now, she only stared at him-not the grey mist at the door-but the blackened smear that had turned into a man. Suddenly the man's face flooded with features of an apologetic and accommodating nature.

"I'm so sorry" The man spoke.

"What is it, s-sir?" Kim deliberately forced the words to come out into her flickering voice.

"Kim," The man began with the same apologetic expression "you were such a good daughter."

"S-sir, what are you talking about? Who are you?"

"Don't you remember me, Kim? Don't remember the yearly office gatherings? Mr Nguyen would always bring you as his plus one."

"What are you talkin' about? I'm...I..." The receptionist began, but she could barely keep track of the words that came out of her mouth. She was forced back into her consciousness, after being ushered into the comfort of her unconscious mind. It was almost as though a beautiful palace, gifted to her, was being demolished by the very person who had given her the gift. Before she could continue, however, her confusion was interrupted by overtly melodramatic sentiments.

"Oh Kim. I still can't figure out how to tell you. You were always so close to him. You always loved him so much. But...so did I. Mr Nguyen was more than I could have asked for in a mentor. He was like a father to me! Remember me, Kim? David Liu? Uni senior? Later found a job under you dad?"

"A personal connection is essential to break through the impact of the Blursion, fellow reader. I need to inhibit it by exciting the neural pathways in coordination to memory and nostalgia. How can I do that without knowing a single detail about the person in question, you may ask. Well, the trick is to utilise the effect of this Tartarean sedative against itself. Blursion's job is to heighten the electrical stimuli in the creative side of the brain. Once in action, the Blursion leaves the pragmatic side of one's consciousness weakened and inactive. Memory retention and logic becomes ((UNFORTUNATELY PUN INTENDED-THE STYGIAN HAS A NASTY SENSE OF HUMOUR)) blurred. Under thesedative's influence, the brain only actively focuses on synthesis and genesis of ideas. How does that help a Tartarean agent? Well, think about it fellow reader..."

"Dave...Is it r-really you?" The receptionist asked, oblivious to the fact that there never was a David Liu in her life. "B-but you look so...different."

"Age hasn't really treated me kindly, Kim." The man at the other end of the desk replied. "But now is not the time for chit-chat. Kim...your dad...Well, uh, Mr Nguyen wasn't feeling too well this morning. He really tried. He kept grasping onto his breath until the very last moment. But..."

"No...no."

"His heart gave in. I'm...so sorry Kim."

"Did you have a guess at it, fellow reader? Well, all the mind needs, under the Blursion's influence, is a hook. Yes! A hook! A tiny fragment of inspiration-a comment or a word or phrase; and then...the mind spirals into a violent rush. A rapid and constant stream of ideas flows through the mind-active genesis and synthesis. No logic. No memory."

The receptionist could barely stand on her feet. She reached out to the man on the other side of the desk. She almost fell into his arms, as tears started formulating at the edge of her eyes. As she hugged her old friend tightly, the white of her eyes leaked out as drops of sadness and rolled down her reflective dimples. She was right. The man was holding a phone behind his back. At the moment, in the midst of sadness, she realised that the man was violently typing away at his phone.

"And that is how we can use it to our advantage, fellow reader. If I can engrave a new hook into the victim's mind, a new inspiration that is extreme, I can force logic. I can kickstart it by inspiring a spiral of new ideas that become so outrageous and illogical that to make sense of it all, the mind forces itself to look back upon memory. And real memories are much more logical than fragments of our imaginations. That's how it works. That's how the effect of Blursion can counter attack itself if one nudges it in the right direction."

"Wait...David, I...I never went to college. And, m-my dad...he passed away when I was three." Kim Nguyen said as she slowly attempted to pull herself away from the hug.

"Don't you want the rain to stop?" The mysterious man asked slowly, still cushioning her forehead against his left shoulder gently, as Kim realised that she had never met a man named David Liu.

"The w-what? W-who are you? Get of me!" The receptionist screamed as she pushed herself away from the man, hitting her own desk, and stagnating to the cold, concrete floor of the hospital. The man stood where he was, as calm as the summer breeze. He had stopped typing secretively. He smiled at her with an expression of triumph and pride.

"Listen. You're the receptionist of Pellington Hospital. You were under the influence of an unauthorised drug, which thankfully now has lost its power over your consciousness. However, the sedative is still in your system, and as long as it is present in your body it will try to regain dominion over your mind. Right now, you need to rest, because in the next 24 hours your body will experience extreme fatigue if you don't." As the man talked, Kim Nguyen suddenly realised that there were several other people in the radius of her sight. All lying unconscious on the ground. The bodyguards. A few other patients. A few doctors.

"W-what happened here? Oh my god! What h-happened to all these people?" Kim screamed as fear and confusion mingled inside her.

"Well, they're all under the influence of the drug. But it depends on how people react. Some people have a natural defence mechanism that they're born with, which allows them to fall asleep so that the spiralling of ideas doesn't have any actualizing impacts on their bodies. Some, however, are unfortunate, and they live consciously through the spiralling, and therefore, for example, if you began having ideas about jumping off of a cliff, you would probably actually jump...wait; Why am I telling you all this?"

Before Kim could react the strange man had already pulled out a strange looking magnet. Kim stared at it. She stared at the man pressing a dainty purple button on the surface of the magnet. She stared at the strange physical oscillations that came from the magnet. She watched as they slowly brought her to the ground. Kim suddenly felt the urge to sleep. She wanted to rest. Before closing her eyes, she glanced at the man who was standing directly above her with a kind expression. She watched him mouth the words:

"Sleep tight, Kim Nguyen."

Then the monochromatic lights of the hospital ceased their childish flickering, and it all went dark. Altogether.

CHAPTER XI

The Standoff

"Ya know sonny, you're startin' ta get me real mad!" A tall, fat man yelled, his words crowded by his thick Italian accent. He wore a designer hat that created the impression of stature and sheer power. His moustache was thick and black, accommodating his gruff and deeply screeching voice. He had turned to a reddish shade of pink out of anger, especially at his dimples-which reduced the daunting impression created by his tailcoat, designer shirt and trousers, and expensive cuff-links and jewellery to a significant degree. He nevertheless continued to yell at his surroundings, and at those who surrounded him. He was surrounded by a group of people. On his side were his men, all of whom wore similar tailcoats, formal clothing, and an array of jewellery-but nothing compared to the man who had turned red. His army of goons carried a plethora of heavy weaponry-automated machine guns, assault rifles, Renetta pistols, sub-machine guns, and bags of hand grenades and smoke bombs tied to their waists-they had come prepared. They wanted to impose superiority, which only meant one thing: the other organisation involved in this gathering was very...very dangerous.

The entire heap of men stood in the middle of nowhere. It was a deserted plane, decorated with undulating sand dunes and the occasional sweat droplets that trickled down from the men's bodies and evaporated rapidly at the devilish touch of the land beneath their feet. The sun was scorching in its glory over the wretched piece of land, its several hundred rays of light reflecting off of the metallic hoods of the several off-road SUVs and heavy pickup trucks surrounding the men. The cars-all of which belonged to the man who had turned red-were also loaded with extreme amounts of heavy and armed weaponry-all except one. The shiniest of the cars, a giant custom-made off-road pickup truck, carried no weaponry and no passengers at the moment. The only thing that it held to its will was an abnormally large box that seemed to be made out of lead. This was to be a promising day.

"Mad? Why, what's there to be mad about?" A voice replied. It was softer in nature, at least compared to that of the gruff and tough octaves of the man who had turned red. It was lightly dabbed with mixed accents of American and British, but nothing too clear or obvious. The voice came from a slender, athletic figure which mainly reassembled that of a man-although no one could ever really tell. The figure, who wore a peculiar looking mask, with an attached golden monocle for his right eye, and nothing for his left, a short hat gently sitting on his head, an expensive branded trench coat, with more expensive branded overalls underneath, and a black watch with embedded gold, was more of a symbol. Even though he was often regarded as a man, he truly had no assigned gender or age. He was more than human-more than materialistic elements of carbon compounds. He could have even been regarded as an 'it'-an animal, a hungry, yet coldly calculated greyhound, who had no problem in killing off other members of his pack for a larger supper. This masked being encompassed sheer power...power that could turn the world around, making it dance on one's fingertips. His aura was unwavering. He stood calm and composed, knowing fully well that the other party involved in this gathering was slowly edging towards the thought of war. He did not care. It did not care. Maybe this masked animal had seen this same story play out so many times, and come out of each of those stories untouched and without a scratch. Sometimes, the intermingling of experience and power gives you a sense of confidence that could match Heimdall's foresight.

"Listen t' me! Our deal was simple. Ya let my men and me in, and then we give ya the weapon of mass destruction and what not. Now you're tellin' me that you're unsure whether or naat it's possible to let m' guys in. Are you stupid o' somethin'? We came awll th' way from..." The fat man spoke angrily in his mangled accent, but his words were cut short.

"Shh shh shh," The masked man quickly silenced the fat man, and continued "Boccioni...you and your men are incredibly brave. We are aware of the lengths you have travelled and the measures you have taken for this...well...fruitful meeting, but The Stygian-we only accept the elite few. You are...too good...for our kind. The overlords think that it is the best for all of us, if you continue to lead all the mob families in New York, and we shall continue to provide you with delights such as immunity, police protection, and power over the local state officials-well...as long as you guard the location, and let us conduct our businesses smoothly. What do you say?"

"Listen ta me, wise guy...neva...silence me...eva again. Got it?" The fat man's voice became deathly quiet, as he continued "As for ya stupid deal, I want ta call it off. My men ar' done protecting your shady business, and as fa' as I can see, I don'' get much outta this. I already got half the NYPD under ma belt. I drink cawffee with ma guys from Congress everyday, an' the other crime families send me birthday cawrds every Tchewsday! So what on gawd's earth is the big idea here, huh? We're done! Ya can take them cards and those special currencies and shove 'em up..." Mob boss Boccioni suddenly stopped dead in his tracks. He realised that everyone was pointing guns of all kinds at him, everyone...including his own men.

The masked man facing him stood plainly with his hands in the pockets of his trench coat. Several suited army men, SWAT team agents, goons, suited marine corps agents, navy seals agents, and uniformed officers-their uniforms riddled with several different flags of various different countries-stood behind him, pointing all their guns at Boccioni. The men on Boccioni's side, goons of the Italian crime family, also stood in their positions pointing their guns at him. The reddish shade of pink on the fat man's face turned to crimson. Anger slowly turned to...fear.

"You know, Boccioni," The masked man began. "My mother always told me a very peculiar bedtime story, when I was younger. See, it goes something like...well, once...there was this wolf, who lived alone in the lonely woods. He was the only large predator in those woods, so he thought himself to be very powerful. He would constantly go around torturing young maiden birds, and smaller creatures such as helpless rabbits, and poor squirrels. He would toy with them, make them commit the worst of atrocities before eating a few from the very large population of animal slaves that he had built. The slaves never sought out to live a better life again, and the wolf continued to passively harass them as time went on. However, the wolf was a little thick in the head. See Boccioni, this wolf was so lonely that soon he mistook his slaves for his family. Started to believe that his slaves were 'his men' and that they worshipped him because they truly loved him. The wolf was wrong. The slaves were simply scared. So, when a new family settled in the farmhouse close to the woods, the slaves were suddenly rekindled with hope. This family worked in the farms all day, and had several other animals working in equal unison with them. In particular, this family had a large bull, a smaller cow, a few sinewy goats, several black sheep, and two buffalos-all of whom were led across and around the farm by a black greyhound. These animals worked very well together and were loved by the family. So every day after work, the group of farm animals would roam the meadows playing around. One day, when the big, bad wolf was sleeping all the wild animal slaves ran out of the woods and approached the farm animals. They begged and pleaded with the farm animals to help them defeat the wolf. The greyhound, who always had a plan, went and discussed the situation with the family. To avoid conflict the family suggested that it would be a good idea to domesticate the wolf and let him also become a partial part of this family, so that he would go easy on his slaves. So, the farm animals went and spoke to the wolf, who at the time was overjoyed by the proposition of no longer being lonely. He was given the privilege of ruling over the other woods surrounding all the farms owned by the family. Can you guess how that came to be, Boccioni?"

The Mob boss was too stunned to speak.

"Well, the family sent their strongest asset to convince the rulers of the other woods to give kingship to the lonely wolf. None of them-A giant Mountain Hare, a huge Brown Bear, and a hawk-like

Pheasant-wanted to give away their kingship. So...the greyhound went and torched those woods. He saw the animals and their rulers cry out of pain and terror, and he stood there with no remorse, no guilt but only determination. Afterwards, the other farm animals worked and grew back those woods into replenished forests, and all of it was given to the wolf. The wolf thought he still ruled over his so-called 'family', but by then they had been bought off and saved by the farm owners and the farm animals." Concluded the masked man.

"Beautiful story, no...Boccioni? Well, I am going to kill you off, now. I am going to take the nuclear waste that you think is a weapon of mass destruction...which it is not. Unfortunately, you'll not be able to see it when we do turn your precious nuclear waste, all of which you have been collecting from your corrupt 'guinea pig' factories that-we gifted you-into a true weapon of mass destruction. You were just a pawn...weak...insignificant...irrelevant."

"B-but why?" Boccioni finally chokingly got the words out.

"Well, think of it like this...the farm owners believe in nomadic agriculture. So sometimes...to get better crops...you need to watch the world around you...BURN."

"Wh-how...wait, wait...maybe we can keep the deal afta' all-I'm sawrry. Listen..."

"Oh, Boccioni, one last thing...if you were wondering-I did end up taking my mother's life. Haha...funny actually. Alright...kill him."

"Wait wait wait wait...NO NO NO!" Boccioni screamed and cried out loud, but it was too late. Several thousand guns shot several thousand bullets at the fat man's body and it jittered in a dying frenzy. The shots were fired for six, deafening rounds. A guaranteeing endeavour few might say. By then the body had turned limp, and soon it fell to the floor with a quiet thud. A dark red liquid leaked out onto the heated floor of the land, and seeped through the cracks in the dried soil and sand.

"Okay." The masked man began. "We take the vehicles back to Hell's Kitchen. Alpha team, start now, and set up ground surveillance as soon as you reach the...location. Beta, are the falcons ready?"

"Yes sir." A group of SWAT team agents responded.

"Good. Initiate cloud surveillance. Eagle 1, are we good to go?"

"Sir, yes sir!" A group of Marines responded, while saluting.

"It is all coming together. Soon...it will be time for dominion. Well, what are you all waiting for? Get me that lead box. Let's go Eagle 1. Team Beta, Gamma, and Theta you will accompany our newly formed alliance members here on their trucks and SUVs. We will all meet at the location, and together...we shall conduct the gate-opening ceremony for this new and final chapter of our mission. For The Stygian. For Tartaroux!" The masked man finished, however, promptly on of the suited soldiers briskly walked up to him and whispered something into his ears. Most of the militia groups controlled by the masked man had already embarked on their journey, wasting no time in following their master's order. It was on the army helicopter that had just landed in the middle of the dessert, that waited for the masked man, along with a few troops closest to him.

"And this information is not corrupted? It's credible?" Asked the masked man, completely expressionless. "Because if this turns out to be false, and our ceremony is delayed because of your hunch...then I'll cut your body into little pieces and then feed them to...the several different creatures we have in trusted labs around the world." The masked man finished staring at his troop. The troop simply gulped. His legs had begun shaking and he took a few steps back away from the masked man, however, he continued to nod frantically, suggesting that he indeed was telling the truth.

"Well. I believe you." The masked man began. "If the coin and the box have been stolen, then I'm glad those idiot brothers are dead. However, we need to get going, and fix this...*temporary issue*. Figure out the location of the stolen artefacts, and get a special task force ready. All equipment is eligible, because the artefacts can be anywhere. We need them for the ceremony. I...need them!"

Dawn had just begun to unfold. The night sky gently dissociated into a paler nothingness, before reappearing white as snow, almost like a beautiful empty canvas, which was priming itself to be painted on by the several hues of sunlight that were to come. The artificial light which illuminated the night life of London began flickering, and one by one-from individual lamp posts to entire commercial sky-scrapers-the monochromatic leviathan lost its minute cells of manmade light, and soon was overshadowed by the angelic glow that came from the bright yellow blotch at the centre of the sky canvas.

"**6:00 AM**" the alarm clock on Hemant's bedside table read. However, he was not in his bedroom. In fact, Hemant Shah had not been in his bedroom for a very long time. His body lay flatly on the marble floor of his living room, as he gazed outside his window. A small, grey suitcase lay beside, several pieces of clothing sprawled across its hollow surface. A few pieces of underwear, socks, and ties littered the floor that connected the living room to the dining hall, where a laptop stood upon, on the kitchen island. The tap showered droplets of water onto the metallic sink on the kitchen island, one droplet at a time, which created a dull rhythm of painfully slow tempo. Hemant appeared to be dazed. His skin was not as pale as it had been for the last five years. His pupils contracted further and further as he focused on a singular thought: They were dead. The Alverez brothers had perished, that too moments after Hemant had bid them adieu.

The laptop on the kitchen island bore the news in large fonts:

" *THE UNTIMELY DEATH OF THE JEWELLERY COMPANY OWNERS: A TRULY UNFORTUNATE RENDEZ-VOUS WITH LONDON, FOR EDUARDO AND THIAGO ALVEREZ AFTER THEIR FIVE-YEAR LONG RETREAT IN MEXICO* "

How was this possible? How? Hemant had left them completely fine. Sure, he broke a pinky-toe, but that was all. Death is much more of a stretch. They were alive, speaking, thinking-and now they were in body-bags. Hemant felt feverish. He contemplated having done the deed. What if that unbreakable spirit that took hold of him in room 606 compelled him to commit to something that he could not fathom. Was it possible? Could something as metaphorical as the spirit of Quilton Addams have controlled Dr Shah to do something that he now regretted. What scared Hemant more was the fact that the head detective inspector leading the case entered the room right after him. Was James Rex welcomed by the death of the Alverez brothers when he entered the room. If so, then how did Hemant manage to escape? Hemant recalled the events of the previous night as he remained flat on the ground. He had walked to the subway station feeling tremendously accomplished. He remembered being zealous about travelling to New York, to finally discover what this "black and white world" was. He walked home leisurely, and then took a bath. He could not sleep. He was too excited. He started packing his research material and his clothes, and finally at 5 in the morning, the news flashed across the screen of his trusty laptop. The police force had more than 12 hours to find him and arrest him. What was holding them back? This tardiness from the force was proof enough that Hemant was not a suspect, that he could not have done it, that it was impossible for him to commit to something so grave and then completely block it out of his memory, while being under the influence of 'some spirit'.

Hemant chuckled slightly as he felt a tingling sense of reassurance climb its way along his spine. However, a new sense of fear soon arose. If it was not him, then who killed the brothers? The cop! Could it be?

A sudden clash of noise jolted Hemant back into reality, and he sprung out of the way, as a figure leaped at him through the window that Hemant faced mere seconds ago.

Hemant tumbled and fell on his sofa, confused. He looked up slowly, while gently lifting his palm to the back of his head, which was now throbbing with persistent pain. His window had been shattered completely, a large hole gaping at its centre. The wood-carved design on the window's interior had been pried open through the sheer force with which the figure burst in from the outside. Hemant turned to look around. Adjacent to the horribly, disfigured window stood a tall figure. Its silhouette emulated an aura of command and power, and Hemant felt goosebumps, as he imagined the figure silently gazing at him. However, a doctor's mind is often plagued with pragmatism and inquiry, and so despite being caught off-guard, Hemant's mind quickly raced to reach the only plausible theory at hand.

"Addams! You know you could have just rung the bell. And why on earth are you wearing a mask and a cloak and all that fancy stuff? I already know what you look like." Hemant exclaimed, as he felt his feet helping him back up on the floor. Surprisingly, the mysterious figure looked slightly taken aback. He stared at Hemant for a little longer and then he spoke.

"Now, who in the bloody hell is Addams? Penfeather, are you alright? And why on earth are you still wearing that costume?" A gruff yet gentle voice spoke with a slightly bewildered tone.

"Penf...what? Addams what are you saying? What happened to your voice? Wait, have you got a voice changer under that cloak?" Dr Shah responded, who now was bewildered as well.

"Don't play them games with me Penfeather, you know exactly who I am. Or have you forgotten your old partner, huh?"

"Wait, that voice!" Hemant exclaimed "It can't be! Detective Inspector?"

"Looks like memory hasn't betrayed you yet, mate." The figure spoke, as he lifted the cloak off his head. Now Hemant saw those hawk-like eyes staring into his soul once again.

"What on earth is going on!" Hemant yelled as he spoke "Inspector why have you busted my window, and what are you wearing? Who is Penfeather?"

"Oh, so you want to play civilian, huh? I'll bust that face as well if you don't take off that hideous mask!"

"Hideous? Hey! This is my face, you moron! And I don't know any Penweather or Pencilshedder, or Henfodder or whatever it is that you're looking for!"

"Alright, that's it, you insufferable punk!" The inspector in comical attire spoke as he drop-kicked Hemant in the chest. The doctor flew across the room, before crash landing on the kitchen island and rolling off onto the other side, beyond the inspector's visibility.

"OWW! What the hell!" An invisible voice began from the other side of the Kitchen Island. The inspector got up on his feet, and slowly walked to the dining hall.

"Come on out Penfeather. This brawl has been awaiting us for a while!" The inspector yelled confidently, as anger took hold of him. No one spoke back from the other side. The doctor's apartment suddenly turned dead silent. The inspector, however, remained unfazed, and focused on the kitchen island.

"Come on, Penfeather. This is the oldest trick in the book, haha! What? Are you going to suddenly leap from behind the blindspot, and try to side-kick me in the face? Well, unfortunately I know all your profoundly stupid tricks, already!" screamed the inspector, before guarding the left side of his face with his left elbow, standing in a defensive stance of the standard Muay Thai fighting style. He expected to feel a jolt across his left elbow, which would mean that he had successfully blocked the attack, after which he would duck, and then throw a haymaker at the target's face. He used to use this strategy in the academy all the time, and had established its efficacy in real life standoffs with actual criminals, during his years of service in the force. The sheer excitement of finally defeating his opponent made detective inspector James Rex's body twitch uncontrollably. However, soon he realised that nothing had happened yet. He did not feel anything along the lining of his elbow or his forearm. In fact, he had felt nothing for quite a few moments. The inspector suddenly looked up and turned around.

"Holy mother of God, Penfeather! Are you trying to run away? Yelled the inspector out of bemused frustration.

Hemant Shah, who was attempting to twist the doorknob of his front gate as quietly as possible, suddenly flinched. He guiltily looked back at the inspector and gave out a fearful chuckle, before yanking the door open as fast as he could. Hemant sprung out of his apartment and tried to make his way to the elevators along the floor corridor, but just after two hard steps out into the open, his body was pulled back in. The inspector grabbed onto the doctor's collar as he tried to run, and pulled him back into the room before flinging the doctor's lanky body across the hall, at the flat-screen television in the living room area. Hemant fell to the ground with a loud, embarrassing thud, which was followed by a softer thud of the broken television collapsing on top of him. James Rex gently closed the main door of the apartment before locking it from the inside. Now he glared menacingly at his target.

"Oww...God, my T.V. You crazy bastard!" grumbled the doctor, as he slowly pushed away his beloved, now demolished television away from him, proceeding to stand up."

"Alright chump, this was good fun, but let's stop playing games alright. Were the brothers useful? Did you get any intel out of them, besides the usual '*oh for The Stygian for Tartaroux*' bull crap? Tell me Penfeather, and we can work this together. You may have abandoned me, but I'm cut from a different metal, I'll keep coming back to work with you, if it means that we put a stop to this insanity. Work with me, Lex. C'mon man!" A flair of brotherhood and loyalty flashed across the inspector's eyes, but it had no effect on the oblivious doctor.

"For the last godforsaken time... I DON'T KNOW ANY PENFEATHER!" Yelled the doctor with all his might-his anger, fear, and pain accumulating to form a sense of frustration like never before. The inspector looked unconvinced. He continued to blabber in gibberish about some group called *The Stygian* and someone called *Tartaroux*; however, it made little sense to Hemant Shah. Finally, after a few minutes, unable to listen to the uncontrolled blabber that automatically helped itself out of the inspector's mouth, Hemant Shah did the unthinkable. In a fit of rage and frustration, the doctor walked up to the inspector in a hasty attempt to make him stop talking. Hemant never was an advocate of practised violence, but in this instance, he could not help but think of punching the outrageous inspector across the face. So, he did. Well, at least he tried to do so. The detective caught Hemant's right hook with ease, and stared at him with a rather disappointed look. Hemant stared back, anticipating something much worse being reciprocated. As he stared at the scowling face of the detective, trickles of sweat precipitated out of every region of his slender figure, and his clothes were soon stained with dark blotches everywhere.

With one swift movement of the arm, the detective flung Hemant off the floor and smashed his body against a nearby coffee table.

"Alright, let's play." The detective said, as he looked down upon the doctor's body which had just been slammed onto the floor, a shattered coffee table underneath his beaten body. The doctor unable to get up could only look back apologetically at the determined inspector. Hemant assessed the different types of pain he was experiencing at the moment. He came to a very valid conclusion-it was a lot of pain.

"Aw...O-ouch." The doctor let out a hushed cry "Inspector...what has gotten into...w-wait...what are you doing...h-hey, HEY...PUT ME DOWN! No, no, no! ARRGH!"

With another swift movement of the arm, the detective replicating stances from the traditional fighting style of Judo, he picked Hemant up before throwing him back onto the kitchen island. Hemant screamed as his body clashed with a few kitchen utensils, before tumbling over to the other side once more.

"You know, Penfeather, if you're not going to help me, I might as well just arrest you, huh? You have no idea how many government forces have warrants on the books and records about you. Better yet, I might just kill you-because the amount of people who want you dead off the records is significantly higher. I'll make a handsome amount, and then I track down this bloody secret society myself, eh? You down for that, Lex?" The detective yelled at the kitchen island assuming that the doctor was listening to him from the other side. Again, there was no response this time. The detective looked back just to check once. The front door was still locked.

"You're not yourself, Penfeather. What? Are you just going to let me throw you around like this?" The detective asked as he turned a corner to directly face the doctor. Suddenly, the doctor's figure flashed before the detective's eyes, and before he knew it, the doctor had slashed out two massive cuts across the frontal regions of the detective's thighs-one large, bleeding cut on each leg. The detective yelled softly, as the stinging agony began to sink in. James Rex realised that he was losing blood at a heightened rate. He felt light-headed and slowly tumbled to the ground.

The doctor's figure-torn and beaten, with miniscule sticks of the shattered coffee table and tiny glass pieces of the broken television jutting outwards from the surface of his skin-stood over the detective with a bloodied knife in one hand, droplets of crimson streaming down from his nose due to the sheer adrenaline of the moment.

"Arterial bleeding, that...ought...to hurt." The doctor said as he gasped for breath in between words "that too from the femoral arteries-I bet you're feeling...light-headed, huh?"

The detective gasped trying to get up, trying to talk, but he couldn't. He muttered "H-h-how d-did..."

"I'm a doctor, motherf..." Hemant began but before he could finish, the detective's vision and his hearing betrayed him as he collapsed entirely.

He did not get up again. Hemant Shah stood there, a sense of bafflement rejoining his consciousness once more. Why was the detective inspector here? Who on earth was Penfeather? What was going to happen now? More questions, and still no answers. Hemant stared at the inspector's bleeding body for a while; a pool of blood had already taken over the territory surrounding the inspector's body. Suddenly a strange frenzy drove Hemant to quickly lift up the inspector's body and place it on a chair. Very quickly Hemant began treating the deathly wounds that he himself had gifted the detective. Hemant knew that he had to save this man, not because of his goodness, no Dr Hemant Shah had been pushed way beyond his limit to have a moral compass any longer. Hemant wanted to save this man because he desperately yearned for answers to his innumerable questions.

As Dr Shah operated with a surgeon's frenzy on the detective, with the limited number of materials he had at his disposal, a peculiar idea tardily metamorphosed into an even more peculiar theory inside the confinements of Hemant's mind; and he was left gaping at the inspector's still body, quite frankly unable to fully fathom what he had just thought about, while his hands continued to treat the detective through the sheer power of impulse and muscle memory.

Soon, however, it all started to make sense. Hemant knew what he had to do. Hell's Kitchen would have to wait just another day; first he needed to question the inspector about a man named Quilton Addams, or perhaps about his other alias...Lex Penfeather!

CHAPTER XII

An Overdose Of Delirium

"Time's running out rather quickly. But everything seems to be going according to plan. Once a guinea pig...always a guinea pig, fellow reader. See you soon, Rex."

For a few moments it was pitch black. No sound. No light. The reign of totalitarian darkness. However, consciousness soon began eating away at this darkness. It began with a flash of light that separated into several redshifted spectrums before disappearing entirely. This was followed by the sound of water dripping from a tap somewhere nearby. As detective inspector James Rex slowly abandoned his immobile demeanour, which had been persistent for a couple of hours, he began to actively assess his situation.

Fascinating is a detective's mind-his consciousness.

It took the inspector little time to regain his thinking, before his mind began racing-flooding its host with speculations, observations, and questions. Similar to how the doctor's hands worked in involuntary autopilot during a surgery, the detective's mind could kick start perhaps even after death- without the need for care or cure. James Rex's mind, intuition, and reflex was refined to the extent where he could solve problems without being conscious. Such was the power of a detective's speculative and inquisitive intuition; and moreover, this was no ordinary detective. James Rex was the smartest in the room since his preschool days. Then smartest in the class. Then smartest in the college hall. Then smartest in the police academy. Now, smartest in Dr Shah's apartment...tied to a wooden chair, unable to get up or fight back. It was only his mind that ran the race across the neural circuits that intertwined in and around his brain.

"So...you're awake." A voice spoke. The detective could barely look up; but he knew to whom the voice belonged.

"Tsk tsk tsk...ah ah!" The voice warningly whispered. "You've been sedated for hours. Don't try. It will be very difficult to move, considering the fact that you've just regained consciousness...but I know you can talk. So...I have a few questions...sir."

The neutrality of the tone slightly confused the detective. He continued his effort to look up, but his body just would not give into his thoughts.

"What do you want...to know?" Asked the detective helplessly. He expected some mocking. He expected a few slaps and punches across his face. This was not his first time being held hostage. The detective's extensive...portfolio...guaranteed the fact that he had immense knowledge of several different criminal endeavours...some of which came from brutal experiences. However, contrary to the detective's expectation, the individual in front of him fell to his knees. James Rex was perplexed. Moreover, now the detective could see tears streaming down the doctor's face. Not tears of sadness or pain- but tears of confusion, exhilaration, and delirium. Upon witnessing this strange reaction, the detective took it in his stride to finally look up and inspect the situation.

The doctor kneeled down in front of the detective...slowly lifted his head up. An unnaturally wide grin on the doctor's face gruesomely contradicted the stream of tears diving out of his pupils. A horrific expression it was. The detective, although not fazed by it, seemed concerned. He was after all a man who cared about the well-being of law-abiding citizens.

"Tell me...how can I help you?" asked Detective Inspector James Rex with the tranquillity of a hermit, despite the fact that he was the one tied to the chair.

"I had a few questions about this Lex Penfeather," The doctor began, his tranquil voice not even remotely matching the horrific, grinning expression. "I know a man named Quilton Addams and, well I think they're the same person, so...uh...is my face looking a bit odd to you? It almost hurts. I don't know, it feels strange."

"Yes, erm..." The detective began, as he pondered how he would articulate his next sentence. "You currently seem to be unaware of the fact that you're literally crying and grinning like a madman at the same time, I think. Right?"

"What? No...I don't know. I was just so fixated on getting answers. The confusion! I CAN'T TAKE IT ANYMORE!" The Doctor's calm voice suddenly transposed itself into a deafening bellow. The detective's eyes suddenly glowed up, and he looked straight at the doctor.

"How long have you been...uh seeking *answers*, if I may ask?" The detective tried to keep his voice as low as and easy-going as possible.

"I don't...I...Arrrghh! I don't know! I don't know! I met him a while ago. Then—then I forgot, then I...I remembered the—the b-black...Yes! The black and the white! That's what he had talked about. Quilton Addams! The man with an expensive trench coat, and a sub-metallic bag that has something red over it—which is not tomato sauce! I REMEMBER!" The doctor mumbled away to glory, clearly lost in a strange trans. His calm composure that had helped him neutralise the angry detective and then prevent him from bleeding to death had completely abandoned him. Right now, in front of a calmer Detective Inspector James Rex, lied the husk of a man who had been imprisoned by his curiosity for months. That feeling of '*something*'—neither excitement nor the feeling of newness—that Hemant felt every time he thought about the man with the alias of Quilton Addams and this *black and white* was much too unbearable now. He could not take it anymore. His emotional quotient had been entirely drained.

"Oh boy...you know him too, don't you?" responded the detective as a stream of thought as clear as day finally swam across the horizon of his mind.

CHAPTER XIII

A Chat In The Cafe

The Heathrow airport was as loud and bustling as ever-families, couples, solo-travellers, and businessmen all walked over the reflective tiled floors like a colony of frantic ants. The month of April brought the beautiful season of spring back, although London was not keen on celebrating it. The sky was riddled with melancholic clouds that drifted in silent solitude, which may have also been the reason for a spike in international travel around this time. People wanted to spend their holidays in the tropics with warmth and tranquillity. Well, most people. Few people, of course, were on the verge of finally solving a treacherous mystery.

"So...what you're telling me is that this man, whom you know very little about as well, has been secretly dosing me with an array of psychedelics—some of which haven't even been made public by scientific associations around the world, including some drug called Dellirictus—which have been tampering with my memory, my perception of reality, and increasing the sense delirium so that I continue to pursue the idea of their being some sub domain of the black and the white!" spoke a man with neat black classes, a nut-brown skin, and tree bark-brown eyes—his right hand attending to a cup of cappuccino, and his expressions bringing forth hysteria. Across the table, in front of him, sat a man with pitch black pupils, and a perfectly groomed beard, who looked back at his companion with an apologetic expression.

"I mean...there is a black and white world, and it is less a sub domain and more of an underground civilization of elites who have embarked on a mission to harness the sun's energy." The bearded man said approaching.

"So...they want to be like a...type 2 civilization?" The doctor replied a little more calmly.

"Precisely."

"And you expect me to believe all this, when in fact you tried to kill me over the idea that our shared acquaintance had two aliases?" The doctor spoke, this time with a tinge of malice in his voice.

"Yes, yes that was very stupid and ignorant of me, and I am terribly sorry; can we move on already?" The detective replied with slight annoyance. "You seem much calmer now. My remedy is working, eh?"

"Didn't even know there was a drug that could induce delirium, let alone cure it. But yeah, it seems to be working...a little too well, and I can't imagine a drug that neutralises the effect of an uncharted, advanced psychedelic hallucinogen like the Dellirictus to be healthy for my body." The doctor retorted back, getting even calmer in his expressions.

"What do you mean 'too well'?"

"Well, until now, you've told me that this man whom I've faintly known as Quilton Addams and whom you've known as Alexander Penfeather, first met you at the academy. You've told me that he was always unique in the sense that he was phenomenal at everything he did?"

"Exactly so. On our first day, he was the first one who managed to tackle down the drill sergeant by using his own technique—something that was taught to us moments before we were challenged. It was frankly impossible for anyone to memorise the moves exactly and then incorporate them into our wrestling styles—but Lex did it!" The detective replied with a fondness that nostalgia brings within people.

"You say, he was the 'first'? Who else managed to tackle your drill sergeant?"

"You're looking at him, kid!" The detective boasted. His eyebrows rose up to shorten the width of his shiny forehead, and his eyes widened, as his lips curled into a slightly arrogant smirk. The detective slowly and steadily lifted his cup of hot americano, and took in a loud slurp of coffee. The sunlight had grown brighter as dawn turned to midday, darting through the glass windows of the airport that overlooked the runway, which harboured several international aeroplanes with a plethora of brands and labels riddled across their surfaces. They were finally here. They were finally going to Hell's Kitchen, New York. Amidst their eccentric conversation that brought much clarity to Dr Hemant Shah, and brought a sense of closure to DI James Rex, both men found a strange banter suspended within their environment. Both men felt a sense of comfort, knowing the fact that both of them now knew all that they could have known. This strange mystery was finally coming to an end. Both the doctor and the detective were sure of it.

"You do realise that I'm older to you." replied the doctor with nonchalance that almost immediately disgruntled the detective.

"Yeah...the Phylocourd is definitely working." The detective remarked as he looked at his companion.

"That's a horrible name for a newly discovered psychedelic antidote. Anyway, you've also told me that you and Addams were drafted on a special police task force, which ended up getting cancelled or something... and then what? Because the incredible Alexander Penfeather couldn't work on a task force, he got mad and then...just vanished?"

"Yeah. No one really thought much of it at first and we didn't really care. But, when I look at it now, I guess joining that task force was really important for him, because he somehow already knew what that task force was meant for; I know the rest of us didn't, and that's why me and the lads couldn't care less. But Penfeather, he...he was disappointed. It was almost like some big plan of his was ruined. So, he left, and he made sure to ditch all and any contact with all of us and anyone he'd ever met during his time in the academy. But then he resurfaced, and the first thing he did was getting in contact with me; and—and he just randomly appeared at my front door one day with a back of chips and some beer. Fed me stories of all kinds about an underground civilization divided into two-the black and the white. Pretty simple concept-Ying Yang, Good against Evil, Tomato Potaato- whatever you wanna call it. He brought back with himself the tales of two sides that were desperate to change the world-to develop new technology, to discover new lands, to become something more. A certain group that chose to conduct such endeavours without interfering with the rest of the world–the rest of the world being the 'grey people' according to Lex –and another group that believed that the extermination of these 'grey people' would make it easier to conduct such endeavours–to discover new milestones and evolve into something more. I was fascinated. I was officially hooked."

"So, he's a conspiracy theorist–like those flat-earth folks?" Asked the doctor as comfortable in the cafe chair as he would have been tucked into his bed. This question of course further enraged the detective.

"Not really...no. See, I had a similar reaction to yours when I first spoke to him as a newly established detective years ago. It seemed to me like a movie, or a terrible prank. However, most of all I was terribly confused. Everything that he told him should not have seemed credible or real, yet I had this gut feeling that there was an element of reality embedded into his eccentric comments. And he brought proof: thousands and thousands of pages scrawled on with writings, copied scriptures, diagrams, and even drawings..."

"His journal–that's how he started writing?"

"Exactly! All those movies and books about secret organisations and conspiracies–they are Lex's notes! That's why I was so interested. It was simply bewilderment! I had always been excited by these stories of secret groups of people, of secret lands and locations, even when I was a lil' moppet, I couldn't help but read books and look at videos about these conspiracies–and then I grew up. I put all these ideas to sleep because I couldn't imagine them to be anything outside of creative and genius fiction...but then I found all that I had known in Lex's words, in his writings–and then those sleeping ideas woke up again. They rekindled like fire! Secret organisations, people with dual identities, secret lands–uncharted and undiscovered–all of it frantically scrawled onto paper. I knew where I was going. I knew that I could not trust this bloke–but curiosity man, that'll make you do anything."

"Don't you think, maybe the idea that this writer can get you back your childhood is why you're so determined to aid him. Is it not because you want to relive the simplicity of those times, for which now you continue to drag yourself further and further into this complexity?" The doctor asked with a look that amalgamated the philosophical and the melancholic.

"Remind me again, are you a doctor or a psychologist?" The detective retorted back, unable to hide his outrage at the dissociated reaction. The doctor could not be bothered to the slightest. He simply looked at his companion once more with an insouciant look.

"Point taken, man. Why don't you continue?" The doctor suggested as he took a long-drawn sip from his cup of coffee.

"Initially, he made those notes to convince someone to aid him in stopping the..."

"Stygian? The group of people who wanted to exterminate normal, regular individuals?" The doctor interrupted, but thought it better to stay quiet afterwards, looking at the dishevelled reaction of the detective. He raised his hand apologetically and let his companion continue once more.

"Yes. However, he came to me not in desperation, but with a strange, relaxed demeanour. It was strange because it was not, and I know this sounds insane, but what really made my hair stand back then, was the fact that this insanity seemed to fit perfectly into Penfeather's personality. It seemed as though his time off the grid had not changed him one bit. He was just as strange as he had been in the academy—only now he came back to me blabbering about this underground elite civilisation. He didn't need my help because I was the only one to help him. He came to me for a story. He just wanted a new character for his journals.

That's not all, however. Even in the academy he was unpredictable—flaky, and spontaneous. We never really knew what he was up to and he would rarely ever tell us. But it was evident that he carried a lot of information in his messed up little head—even before he had gone off the grid, even before that task force was discussed, we always knew that Alexander Penfeather was not going to stick around to become a police officer. Joining the academy was like a day camp for him. A small task to refine his skills, and then he would leave. We knew that his 'training' must have begun way before he joined our academy.

"What do you mean? And just don't ramble. Be a bit more definitive." Replied the doctor, still completely unimpressed under the influence of Phylocourd. The detective was now visibly annoyed. A group of people swiftly entered the airport cafe, and began lining up against the counter. It was almost time for the flight that would land in the La Guardia Airport in New York.

"Quit interrupting me!"

"Well," The doctor began completely ignoring the angsty remark and denying the detective an opportunity to speak once more. "You've also told me that after you both had your romantic rendezvous again a few years back..."

"There was no rendezvous!" the detective interrupted furiously. "Penfeather happened to resurface and he happened to approach me. But I could tell I wasn't the first. He had experience. He knew what he was doing. During his time off the grid, he had been doing nothing but exploring the black and the white."

"Yeah—yeah whatever. Anyway, after you both began working together, he dragged you into the sub-lair of The Stygian? But they had this hierarchy, right? You planned on staying, working as an inside man–you wanted to slowly work up this hierarchy until you were close enough to the overlords of this organisation-just so that you could sabotage their operations? That's incredibly chaotic and unbelievably stupid, might I add–one cop against an entire–in your own words– 'underground civilization of elites who have embarked on a mission to harness the sun's energy'."

"I...well...yeah..." The detective began but his embarrassment evidently manifested itself as two red blotches on his cheeks. "But there was no *sub-lair*. It was like a regular life, except now you knew that there were people everywhere who lived a dual life. People, who called themselves *'Agents of Tartaroux'* or *'Tartareans'*. As a part of The Stygian, they infiltrated the *Grey World*, and anchored it to the underground elite civilisation. We never really met higher ranking individuals from The Stygian hierarchy—people who actually belonged to the bloodline of this elite civilisation."

"And that's why he left isn't it? Quilton Alexander Addams Penfeather or 'the writer' had neither the patience nor the bravado to work his way up this hierarchy, or do his time alone as a member of the organisation that he was willing to destroy?"

"Yeah. But more so it was how much he despised The Stygian. It was almost like he had known about it before he went underground. It was almost as though he knew even before coming to the academy. The way he talked about those people-he had unbridled hate for them–nothing but hate. He wanted to burn the organisation's plans for augmenting the human race and killing of the 'everyday people', dare I say burn the civilisation's bloodline altogether, and destroy them entirely!" The detective said as though he was telling an old wives' tale. Dr Shah even noticed, in his calm and sedated state, a droplet of tear in the detective's eyes due to the sheer exacerbation of the mind.

"No. That doesn't make sense. Quilton Addams is a man of logic. Hate is a rather disadvantageous emotion, which he definitely does not want to be tied to. And why would he hate them? He has no purpose being altruistic. If he's logical then he's selfish, and if he's selfish then why on earth would he care?" The doctor finally broke out of his nonchalance.

"Perhaps, sometimes logic does lead to altruism–if one realises that good for everyone means good for oneself, it becomes much easier to care for the 'greater good'." The detective responded casually. "But, there's the off-chance that our acquaintance is a complete lunatic and he actually just enjoys having this twisted, outlandish motive."

"And about this Stygian? What are they like? And how on earth does killing off certain people lead to better chances of harnessing the sun's energy?" The doctor asked incredulously before regaining his calm composure.

"Well, during my limited time of 2 years within this organisation, I realised that there was a hierarchy, as I've already mentioned. This hierarchy is what connects this underground organisation to the '*Grey World*'. People ranging from petty thieves and narcotics businessmen, to mob bosses, to corporate moguls, to film stars and the list goes on–all can get in on the action. Even certain Jewellery shop owners. It is rather difficult to get in if you're the average person, but if you somehow manage to do it–you are ensured the Tartarean guarantee that you will not be exterminated. You get special currency. You get a card, and most importantly you get power. Some of the members don't even know about the ulterior motive of wiping the globe into a clean slate by killing off the others–they're just in it for the influence and power. The 'killing off' thing, I don't know, man. I could never understand the logic, even though I tried. Maybe less people would equal less energy consumption, which would give a better chance to do what The Stygian wants to do. Maybe if the regular people were exterminated, there would be more resources to continue developing advanced tech...these are all plausible ideas–but they all seem farfetched and outlandish–and of course very few people in The Stygian truly know what is going on." The detective answered earnestly.

"And that is why, I think that this antidote is working a little too well. All this should make my stomach churn and make my heart pound, but I seem to be accepting it for what it is. It doesn't bother me." The doctor said plainly.

"You're not used to not being bothered, are you?" Asked the detective, as he looked at his watch.

"I'm just...I don't know. Why me?" The doctor began, "He had you, and you're suggesting that he has had several other acquaintances off the grid–which means there are people much more skilled than I ever will be. Why would he need some random doctor to take down this elite, savage organisation." The doctor asked. The detective smiled plainly, before taking another sip of his Americano, which had now turned rather cold.

"Maybe doctor, he just needed another new character for his journals. Maybe you're not special at all, and he simply needs you to make his endeavours more interesting. Contrastingly, maybe you are special. Maybe you have some hidden skill that he knows about. Or maybe...just maybe...all his acquaintances of the grid are impossible to reach or dead, and we are the only two people left, whom he can use without remorse or difficulty." The detective said, deliberately attempting to make his words sound more theatrical and withholding gravitas. The doctor saw right through it. It was evident that the detective was, to a certain level, as confused about this 'writer' as the doctor.

"And this journal writing...how does it work? Why does he still do it?" Asked the doctor, trying to stray away from the concept that both him and the detective were puppets in this strange endeavour of Quilton Alexander Penfeather Addams.

"Mind you doctor, this man is insane. Some of the things he does is simply beyond me; and this is one of those things." Stated detective inspector James Rex earnestly. "However, it seems to me that there is a demand for this kind of writing. There is some audience, some people, perhaps some bloke who's equally unhinged as our dear friend–willing to pay the buck for these details, these–these annotations, diagrams, and stories. And of course, as long as there's a demand–there is most likely going to be a supply."

"So...he's using the secrets of this civilization to fund his attempt to take down this civilization?" The doctor asked in a bemused tone.

"Bloody genius, innit? I mean, although, these days it seems as though he writes everything he experiences–to add an interesting flair of 'docuseries' to his writing, if you will–to make it...uh...seem like an adventure novel."

"Yeah. This guy's definitely nuts! That daft, one-eyed, masked miscreant was right." The doctor mumbled to himself.

"Wait! You've...you've met him?" The detective asked. He had almost spilled his cup of coffee. Even more people had now begun entering the cafe, and the serpentine line of customers at the counter only seemed to lengthen.

"Oh, would you look at that!" The doctor said looking at his watch, "It's time to board. We should go. We're late already." He quickly gulped down the rest of his cappuccino and got up to his feet. The detective still stared at him with a bemused look. Eventually, they both exited the cafe and walked across to the boarding queue. The number of passengers for this plane was relatively small. Most were either attending business or visiting family–at least that's what the doctor could make of the people in his queue.

"You're talking about the guy with a single monocle attached to his mask? No one has ever met him!" The detective whispered. Even Though he tried to maintain a hushed tone–his excitement was evident.

"Besides our shared acquaintance, of course?" The doctor inquired "He told me that he's met him thrice before."

"I don't know about that. All I know is that this masked man calls himself The Feint. He's at the top of The Stygian Hierarchy. You've actually...met him?"

"Yeah." The doctor said calmly. "The man broke my door down to come and meet me. I was sleeping too. He scared me. He put the fear of God in me. He said he would hurt me if I didn't help him bring down Quilton Addams...that Quilton Addams was as dangerous as he was–that he wanted to rid me of this problem that I had gotten myself into..." As the doctor finished, he noticed the detective shooting a suspicious look at him. The doctor smiled.

"I didn't help him. I couldn't. I told Quilton Addams about everything that had happened a day after I had met him, and since then he distanced himself from me. Since then, I have been left in this state of confusion. That's why I wanted to interrogate the Alverez Brothers. They...told me to go to Hell's Kitchen. Well, of course now I know that it was the drug Dellirictus that artificially drove my curiosity to another level, but as you said—Tomato Potaato." As the doctor finished explaining he observed a curious look on his companion; the detective had promptly dived into a deep state of thought.

"Hmm..." The detective began. "Four things. One—If The Feint knows about Penfeather, then the plot of this mystery has only thickened further. It is possible that The Feint only wants to neutralise the man who has been selling the secrets of The Stygian as ideas to people around the world, but it is not unlikely that he knows about Penfeather's desire to burn The Stygian to the ground, and that he wants to kill Penfeather for that very reason."

The doctor's eyes slowly widened as he listened to the detective carefully. He could not care less about the queue for the flight getting shorter as more and more people checked in their boarding passes and walked into the flyover gateway.

"Two...if The Feint broke your doors down a day after you met Penfeather, then he really thinks you're special..."

"But I'm not...I was a nobody until the day I met..." The doctor tried to level with the detective but was interrupted.

"It doesn't matter. If The Feint thinks that you're the best route to get to Penfeather, he will come for you with guns blazing. Perhaps he hasn't done so until now, because Lex decided to leave you behind for long enough to convince The Stygian that you were insignificant."

"Hey...you don't need to say it like that..."

"Which brings me to my third point...if Lex distanced himself from you only to convince The Feint that you were unimportant, then it is likely that he himself does need you—perhaps you're easy to use as a person...or you're interesting enough for his journals. That would explain why he cycled you in and out of uncharted psychedelics—first to make you forget and stay out of The Feint's radar entirely and then to make you remember and pursue this mess once more."

"That's crazy. He messed with my mind because he needed an interesting character for his journal!" Dr Shah whispered hysterically. "Is that what you're suggesting, *detective*?" The doctor maliciously emphasised on the last word of that sentence.

"So...the Phylocourd is wearing off, I see. But yes. He is insane. And this may be a new feat for him. However, maybe, doctor...you are special–at least to him... personally, I can't tell why..."

"You're just jealous that someone you've worked with before gives more of a damn about me!" The doctor said a little louder this time, as he checked in his own ticket, which got him a bewildered expression from the stewardess of the queue. "What was your fourth point anyway?"

"Do you see that man with a strange pair of glasses and an abnormally large moustache?" The detective asked as he glanced at a man who was trying to eat a lemon wedge, which was noticeably wet–most likely picked up from the rim of a used glass in the cafe. The doctor slowly glanced at the man and nodded.

"He's been following us since our time in the Cafe" The detective said. "He's been right behind us the entire time. He's been listening. Stay alert, man."

"Erm...have you considered the fact that maybe he is just boarding the same flight?" The doctor asked mockingly. The detective shot him a nasty look, but never said a thing. Soon the pair made their way into the flyover tunnel, and then eventually into the aeroplane.

CHAPTER XIV

The Man In Medieval Clothing

"This is it. We're at the summit of Gustav's pyramid. We've hit a denouement."

It had been three hours since the doctor and the detective had boarded their flight. For reasons unknown to Hemant, DI James Rex had stopped engaging in any further conversation. He simply sat beside the doctor, snoring away to glory. Hemant noticed James Rex's ebony skin reflecting the gleaming rays of sunlight coming from the aeroplane window beside him. The detective's mouth was wide open, a long streak of dreamy spit splattered across his lower lips. The rest of the plane was predominantly silent. Almost all the passengers had fallen into a deep slumber. It was only the occasional groans of dreamy passengers turning and twisting in their seats to get more comfortable, a few shrill giggles and cries from toddlers, and the frequent messages from the pilot that notified Hemant of the fact that he was not in a ghost plane. He looked out the window.

As Hemant recalled his entire discussion about the strange 'writer' that he had met many months ago, he felt his heart rate increase. The Phylocourd had lost all of its effect. As Hemant let his vision wander about the empty horizon, glancing at the terrains of floating cloud, and the occasional streak of light blue that told him they were still amidst the skies, he realised that he was now stuck in this mess. Moreover, the detective had suggested that it was never his own intrigue that drew him back to this mess, but a devious trick from the writer himself, to keep Hemant captivated—so that he could be utilised. Hemant had been the biggest tool in the last few months. However, that was not what stung him. It was the fact that he was not in control. It was the fact that this rollercoaster that the last few months had been was never his choice. The only choice he had ever made was to talk to the man he thought was named

Quilton Addams. After that he was nothing but trapped. Hemant never had a friend, and as he looked out the aeroplane window, he realised he still did not. He was not a friend to Quilton Addams–he was an instrument–he was simply a prisoner, imprisoned by one terrible choice: acquainting himself with that strange man smoking a cigarette many, many months ago.

"If that's the case then why are you still going?" A familiar voice asked earnestly. It took Hemant a while to realise that someone was speaking to him. He turned his back on the window and looked around. The detective had just woken up, clearly disturbed by the voice that had just spoken to Hemant. He wiped the spit off his face, and looked around blinking as though he had just had a terrible dream. Ignoring the malfunctioning detective, Hemant looked up. It was that strange man with a bizarre pair of glasses that had a swirling design on their surface, and with an abnormally large moustache. He gently smiled at the two companions and sat down at the third seat in their section.

"W-what did I tell you, huh?" The sleepy detective slowly whispered into Hemant's ears. "Never question my skills again."

Ignoring the Detective's snobbish comment, Hemant looked at the man once more. Something seemed familiar about him, but the doctor was unable to determine what it was.

"Uh, sir, I think you have the wrong seat..." Began Hemant, but before he could make his point the strange man retorted with a gentle tone.

"Oh no, I think not. I think I'm exactly where I want to be."

"Well," The doctor began as annoyance took hold of him once more "I quite vividly remember a bald, middle-aged gentleman sitting on that seat, and only mere minutes ago had he left to attend the washroom."

"Oh...him? Well, uh...he's going to be in the washroom for a while." The strange man said in an even stranger way. "I don't reckon he's feeling too well...definitely not after I decked him in the face."

The detective suddenly sat up–his eyes completely and almost immediately abandoning the dreamy expression. His hands suddenly balled up into fists that showed off gnarled knuckles protruding out–almost piercing the skin on top. He looked at the strange man like a predator. The detective's eyes darted all over the strange man's profile–his obnoxious maroon clothes that mimicked an archaic and mediaeval sense of fashion, his swirly glasses, and his jet black, bush-like moustache. The strange man simply smiled.

Suddenly the detective relaxed again–his body plumping down into his seat as he stretched his arms and legs–almost as though he was getting ready for another nap.

"You know mate, you could get arrested for that behaviour?" The detective finally spoke, however, Hemant noticed a weird smirk on his face, like an expression of toddler-like joviality. This childish behaviour from a renowned detective inspector only further annoyed Hemant. He blinked twice and then glared at the detective.

"Man, he's literally confessing to have committed an assault, and *that's* your reaction?" Hemant asked, playing the role of a disappointed parent. The detective simply gave out a chuckle, as he looked at the strange man and then back at Hemant. The strange man simply continued to smile an unsettlingly pleasant smile. His face was much too relaxed for someone who had apparently just knocked someone unconscious. His eyes remained fixated on Hemant–as though he was toying with his food–and soon enough he spoke once more in the same gentle tone.

"Well doctor, you seem to be the only one here who still hasn't the foggiest, so I'll ask again." The man with maroon clothing began, and Hemant's eyes widened as he listened. "If you truly believe that I have gone to such lengths to preserve my connection to you, to make sure The Stygian doesn't come after you, to make sure that you build yourself a fortune before stirring back towards the black and the white, just because in my eyes you're the most useful 'tool' and nothing more than that, then why did you come?"

"Y...no, w-wait..." It took Hemant a little while to fully comprehend the scenario, and furthermore get his words to roll out of his tongue. "YOU!"

"Yeah. Me." Came a very composed response from the strange man, who was now peeling away his thick moustache, which now appeared to be evidently fake, from his face. Soon after he took off the glasses and revealed a familiar face– his perfectly groomed face accompanying his jet-black hair which shabbily hung over his forehead and scattered to the edges and to the back of his head. His devious, light-brown eyes stared at Hemant inquisitively. It was the face of Quilton Addams. It was the face of Alexander Penfeather. Most importantly, it was the face of 'the writer'.

Hemant's eyes had widened to the fullest extent. He was visibly jittering with an infuriated expression. His face had flushed to a shade of crimson, and his feet had begun shaking rhythmically. It was only the hands of the doctor that remained still. He continued to glare at his long-lost acquaintance without uttering a single word. The detective glanced at both of his companions without a word. There was a brief moment of silence, during which the writer stared at the doctor and the doctor glared back unwaveringly. The detective continued to glance around–a clueless viewer watching a silent film.

"D-d'you want another sip of that Phylocourd?" The detective asked, finally cutting through the empty silence of the moment. Unfortunately, that seemed to uncork the bottle brimming with manic suppressed emotions within the doctor.

"No, you idiot! What I want are answers!" The doctor exclaimed, his voice slowly rising.

"But I already told y..." The detective began but his rationale was disregarded and ignored.

"No! Not from you. I want answers from this dimwit! What do you have to say for yourself?" The doctor began, enraged at the sight of his old acquaintance. "If I'm not just a 'tool', then why did you do this? WHY! You could have left me alone. You could have. But instead, you broke into my apartment, and started dosing me with psychedelics, covertly, just so you could use me later! So yes. Yes, I indeed think that I am nothing but a tool to you, and I am here only because you have forced me to be! It was YOU who dozed me with 'synthetic delirium' through one of your strange drugs! You sadistic piece of..." The doctor was forced to thwart his speech, as the detective suddenly clasped onto his neck, and forced a miniscule bottle down the doctor's throat, all the while, the writer simply watched, while the doctor flayed his arms around like a wild beast being forcefully harnessed.

"There...that should do it, brother." The detective said as he pocketed the tiny bottle of Phylocourd back into his jacket.

"You didn't give him more than three drops, did you?" The writer asked, and the detective nodded, although James Rex could not help but detect a sense of concern from the writer towards the doctor.

"Well, doctor..." The writer began swiftly "if you truly wish to return back to your old life, then be it. I have under my belt certain devices that will make you forget all of this. You could go back to your old life without caring about the black and the white. Is that what you want?"

"Yeah, right!" The doctor exclaimed, although under the influence of the Phylocourd he could only merely whisper in outrage. "That's what you said last time, didn't you? And look where that's got me! Knee deep in this bull..."

"No. No more tricks. If you truly don't want to be around then I won't waste my instruments to make you stay. Unfortunately, I had the impression that I had finally found a friend." As the writer spoke, he received an untrusting look from the doctor, and a flabbergasted expression from his old mate from the police academy.

"Of course, other than Detective Inspector James Rex." The writer clarified, glancing back at the detective, who failed to entertain the gibe, and simply slouched further into his seat. A brief noise—similar to that of faint beep—rang out and almost instantaneously died out. The passengers barely noticed.

"I don't know what to tell you, 'Mr writer'," The doctor began, his drug-induced nonchalance returning to him once more. "on one hand I desperately want to dissociate myself from this mess; on the other hand, you've already forced me to come this far. Perhaps, I should finish what you forced me to start with you. I can tell there's an underlying task that you want me to aid you in fulfilling. Otherwise, you wouldn't have shown your face–'cause you're a twit. But that will be it. I won't tag along in this mission to destroy your beloved Stygian, and also–never consider me your friend or even your acquaintance; I'm simply doing this to regain a sense of closure for myself–I owe myself that much."

Upon hearing, the writer remained quiet for some time, however, unbeknownst to him, the detective had noticed a shift in his air–a change in his glance. James Rex simply observed both of his companions from his slouched position.

"Very well. You shall never see my face after this, doctor." The writer stated. "However, now I need you to focus. There's only one reason I chose to meet you again on this plane–and that is because this plane has a weapon–a very prized possession to The Stygian. I need you to help me disarm said weapon. And then you are free to bid me adieu."

Hemant, freshly under the influence of the Phylocourd simply nodded half-heartedly. All the passengers in the plane were still deep in slumber, and it had been quite some time since the last announcement of the pilot. Suddenly that beeping noise rang out again into the vastness of the plane corridors. This time, however, it failed to cease existence. The noise persisted for an entire minute, before coming to an abrupt halt. Several passengers seemed to have woken up due to the strange disturbance, and they continued to look around confused. The lack of any visible staff in the corridors further enhanced the abnormality of the situation. No one spoke. All passengers simply looked around trying to catch a glimpse of any present air-hostess who could bring along some water, or a tray full of meal options, or a pillow to better aid the broken slumber. However, no air-hostess ever came. All passengers simply sat in silence.

"I need you to quietly move to the back of the plane. Do not make any noise, alright? And act normal–casual." The writer said in hushed tones.

The detective looked around the plane, and then looked at his companions with a snobbish air of someone who withheld profound information. "They're here. You idiot, did you know?"

"Maybe." The writer responded. Hemant had reduced himself to a sleep-like state. He was awake–but he could not care. He simply waited for the instructions from the writer.

"Well, who's gonna neutralise *that mess*, while you and 'Bill Nye' here go and fix the mass destruction dilemma?"

"Well, I also needed a reason to have you on the plane. That's why I planned for you to meet the doctor and then unite, and then..." The writer began with an earnest expression, but was met with hushed angst from the detective.

"You planned all this! You've got some nerve. And frankly I'm not in very good shape, thanks to your beloved doctor. He slashed two massive scars on my legs to make sure I bled to death."

"Hey, you tried to kill me." The doctor retorted plainly. "And I did save you at the end. I just needed you to collapse for some time."

"Well, if you two are done bickering, we may begin. Are you done?" The writer asked as he glanced at the semi-sedated doctor and the jejune detective. Hemant simply nodded, while the detective huffed silently.

"Alright." The writer began. "Shah, you're going to follow me to the back. I'll lead you to the device, and I'll instruct you further there. Rex, quit the attitude and focus right now. I need you to hold them off until I'm done..."

"Until *we* are done." The doctor corrected, hoisting up his right index finger, as a sweet substance-induced grin spread across his face. Another, louder beeping noise had just rung out, and this time it was accompanied by a faint bang–its origin, few could tell, being the pilot's cabin. The detective sat up once more. His eyes contracted in hawk-like fashion–like when a predatory bird had finally detected its prey. He brooded for a second before looking back at his companions. His hands had metamorphosed back into balled fists that showcased gnarly knuckles, and his childlike fit had completely faded from his face to leave behind a vigilant, stoic demeanour.

"You need to go. Now!" He exclaimed in hushed tones.

The writer swiftly got up from his seat, and pulled the doctor by his right arm. Completely under the influence of the Phylocourd, Hemant could barely walk without slipping, and he could barely talk without letting out a soft, shrill laugh. The writer had no choice but to support the doctor's partially limp and sedated body all the way to the end of the aeroplane corridor. As he did so he looked at Hemant once more.

"D'you really reckon that...I...only think of you to be a tool? That to me you're only something I can use?" He asked as he looked at his slumping companion.

"A-are we... ARE WE THERE YET?" The doctor yelled dreamily. Several passengers looked around and fixated their judgemental glances onto the strange duo. The writer simply kept on walking, helping the doctor do the same. Neither looked back at the disgruntled passengers.

"Yeah. Rex definitely made you drink more than three drops."

CHAPTER XV

The Lesser Of Two Evils

"Oh God! Please...please, don't do this. I have a wife–I have two kids waiting for me back home. Please!"

"Tsk tsk tsk. You know, my mother always had this beautiful quote that she would remind us of–after she had beaten me and my brothers half to death. After listening to her melodious voice and her pretty words the tears would just disappear off our reddened faces. We would smile and admire her beauty–her intelligence. It went something like..."

"Please! Please God! Oh no..." The co-pilot yelled before breaking down into jittery sobs. His senior counterpart had just pleaded with the several armed men to spare the cabin crew. All of the stewards and stewardesses were tied separately in tight black robes made of an out worldly synthetic fibre that stabbed into the host's skin. Everyone was shaking–tears rolling down the faces of most. The cabin crew was in immense shock and agony. If this was an attempted hijack–it was certainly the most unique. In front of the kidnapped cabin crew stood a plethora of armed men–all in unifying jet-black padded armours. They hoisted several different armed weapons and wore protective gear on their faces to hide their identities. Along with these troop-like gentlemen stood a masked man, with his hands pocketed in his branded trench coat. He stood relaxed and composed as though this was a tea party. All of his clothes were jet-black as well, all except for his mask–which showed off a silver-grey colour, with a singular, golden monocle attached to the right side of the mask, and nothing to the left. He was the one who had been interrupted by the desperate cries of the devastated co-pilot.

"Hmph." The masked man sighed. "You know...I liked you as well. I thought you of all people on this plane would know how to...uh...stay quiet. Ah well, shoot him." The masked man finished, pointing his finger at the co-pilot. Almost instantaneously all the armed men pointed their rifles and pistols at the poor man who was tied–and he too began shaking and screaming with dread. Suddenly, the masked man swiftly hoisted his right hand up in the air, and promptly all the armed men drew their aim away from the shivering co-pilot, who began yelping, unable to process his situation any more.

"Yes...it's that easy for me to have you killed. It's even easier for me to wipe your identity off the face of this planet–so, never...interrupt me. Is that clear?" The masked man asked trivially, his position still relaxed, his hands now back in the pockets of his gleaming trench coat. The entire cabin crew began nodding hysterically, transmitting their verbal distress purely through the means of their broken body language. The co-pilot continued to yelp softly, visibly filled with the relief of not being gifted a 9mm luger to his head, and at the same time filled with the terror of being in the presence of The Feint.

"Now, where was I? Ahh...yes–my beautiful mother's beautiful quote. Yes, of course, I'm paraphrasing but it went something like this:

'You not only see the reality of it all in the final living moments of someone, but also the reality within you.'

Ahh...she was right. When I saw her for the last time–I failed to see the fear in her eyes that I had always craved. I failed to see the painful reality that I hoped would reflect back at me when I killed her. No. All that my mother's reality fostered in that moment–all that I truly saw in her eyes was pride. She, even in her dying moments, and even when I was the reason she was dying, couldn't help but be proud of me! That's when I saw the reality within me for the first time as well. That was the first time I felt immense love for my mother. I cried as I killed her, and she smiled. I lost. She won.

This...well this is quite similar. I see the reality of you all. None of you can care less about each other. All you want to do is survive–to return back to the materials you love: your possessions, your home, your families. That selfishness is what makes us...*human.*

Of course... I see the reality in me as well. I don't feel remorse. I don't feel satisfied. I barely feel anything at the moment other than the faintest feeling of disgust. I'm disgusted at how easily people tend to reduce themselves to crying, shivering, quaking heaps of pathetic at the face of danger." The Feint finished. The gravity of the moment alone had thwarted the streaming tears for several of the kidnapped cabin crew. A few had fainted. The armed men stood behind The Feint—empty robots waiting for their next line of command from the operator.

"Alright. We cannot waste any time. After the brilliant mess up from our gatekeeping subordinates, hmph..." the masked man called The Feint took a moment to sigh before continuing again. "...we need to take matters into our own hands. At the back of this plane lies the device. A device that..."

"That I stole...yeah, I stole this big hunky weapon of mass destruction from the Alverez brothers." The writer stated plainly to the doctor, who now sat on the matted floor of the aeroplane, staring at the strange golden cube of a device with awe. The steeled capsule that the aeroplane was, remained as quiet and still as an abandoned cave. The bright, cyan lights had come alive once more—and the seat belts signs were turned on as well—although there was barely any noticeable turbulence. None of the passengers noticed this key detail, however, none other than the detective inspector...who finally chose to get up from his seat. The pilot's cabin was quite a distance from James Rex's aisle, in the enormous Boeing 777, and the plain, white door was barely visible to the passengers seated in that area. Nevertheless, the detective slowly walked—one step at a time to eventually make his way to the very people whom he had to—in the writer's words—*neutralise*.

Towards the back of the aeroplane, the writer ignored the substance-induced childishness from his partner and continued to explain the situation to the doctor.

"Well, I reckon you've never heard of Obduratium?" The writer asked with a mixture of earnest concern and lampooning snide. It took the doctor a moment to realise that he was being spoken to.

"Huh? Ob...doo...what?" He fumbled, unable to focus on the writer's words, and entirely captivated by the giant golden cube that stood in front of him. The writer glanced back for a moment. It seemed that they were still clear for the moment, however, very soon they would have to face an interruption from certain individuals–the writer could sense their presence. He could smell the smell of callous conflict. He looked back at the doctor. The doctor smiled a dumbfounded smile, and promptly the writer whipped his hand across the doctor's face to slap him as hard as he could.

"Owww! What the..." Hemant began as a familiar sense of angst and rage crawled up his spine.

"That's the only way to lessen the effect of the Phylocourd. Inducing sudden, temporary distress after prolonged exposure to the Phylocourd overrides the inhibitor with stress hormones, which in turn dilutes the efficiency of inhibition." The writer explained, and without taking in another breath he continued at a rapid pace. "Alright...Obduratium. It's an uncharted element. It is the singular impenetrable material on this planet, and its origins are most likely extraterrestrial. It can block any and all particles known to man. Photons, Gamma rays, electrons, protons...and of course, most importantly...positrons."

"Antimatter?" Hemant asked, feeling a sudden change in pace in his atmosphere, and a sense of sheer, curiosity driven excitement. His eyes for the first time in a while contracted and fixated themselves on the writer, and his medically trained, undefeated focus seemed to rekindle once again. The writer smiled gently.

"Precisely. Antimatter from a certain radioactive isotope...which at the moment does not exist."

"Wait. What?" Hemant asked, evidently taken aback by the writer's earnest candidness. He looked up at the writer, and then looked back at the strange golden block. Of course, Alexander Quilton Addams Penfeather simply stood there enjoying the pure awe within the doctor's eyes. There was now evident, audible disturbance towards the other side of the tiny door frame that separated the rest of the aeroplane corridor and the apparent weapon of mass destruction.

"We don't have much time, doctor."

"I really thought you were buildin' up to something there. What d'you mean '*doesn't exist*'?" Dr Shah inquired; his unwavering glance now fixated on the enormous golden block of Obduratium.

"Well, according to my investigations, The Stygian had hired certain people to collect all the nuclear waste from and around New York, and now they're attempting to isolate any possible radionuclide that could emit something other than the classic alphas, betas, and gammas."

"Right. And there aren't any? Not even any *uncharted* ones?" The doctor asked, now being quite familiar with the idea that a lot of things about modern science were likely to be forever undisclosed to the *Grey people*. The writer glanced back at the tiny door, almost ready to kick it down. Hemant could sense a sudden change in the air. Something feral had awoken in the strange man who had once introduced himself as Quilton Addams. The writer stared at the door for a few more seconds. The disturbances grew even louder. Hemant glanced back and forth from the door, to the writer, to the block of golden Obduratium.

"I mean...they'd have better luck with a darned banana." The writer promptly continued their conversation as though his strange blink-off with the tiny door of the back room of the aeroplane had never existed. At the sound of the quip, Hemant involuntarily gave out a chuckle.

"But what do you want me to do?" The doctor asked as he looked at his strange companion.

"Well...obviously you can assume what The Stygian wants to do with antimatter?" The writer asked, almost in a parent-like fashion, his squinting, brown eyes expecting a prompt answer from the doctor, and of course, the doctor did not fail to deliver.

"I would assume they want to purposely fully bring particles and their antiparticles into contact to commence a devastating reaction that would produce enough energy to–what was it that Inspector

Rex said...uh, yeah–to completely *exterminate* the Grey people."

"As anyone would assume." The writer began. "However, if they keep hoping to find the perfect radionuclide that would grace their elite presence with the perfect yield of electron antineutrino to aid their psychopathic plans to kill off an entire unsuspecting legion of innocent people, they would likely never succeed. As I said: they would likely have more luck doing that if they spent their time researching positrons released by the potassium in bananas."

"You calling someone else psychopathic is...deep." The doctor said in with a very visible expression of malicious lampooning, however, the writer swiftly continued with his words–completely ignoring the doctor's jibe, much to his disappointment.

"Well. Now that it is established that The Stygian is not exactly on the right path to destroying the everyday humanity, I want you to suggest an alternate path." The writer finished, staring Hemant dead in the eye.

"What? Why?" The doctor was flabbergasted at the sudden change of pace in their conversation. "What do you want me to say? Why do *you* want an alternate method! Are you..."

"This is the last task doctor. You said you wanted to finish your story here...well, here. Here's your opportunity."

"Hmph..." Hemant sighed, before diving into a state of pure silence. "I...erm...assuming that there is more advanced technology available in this world that I am unaware of– just like the average person–I would probably focus on collecting enough byproduct alpha particles from the radioactive fission of Uranium-238 into Thorium-234, or Uranium-234 into Thorium-230. If I could collect enough to formulate alpha particle bunches for the average particle accelerator, then I would hope to produce anti-alpha particles with said accelerator, and then somehow force a collision between..." Hemant thwarted his speech, looking at the writer whose face now demonstrated a wide, boyish grin.

"Do you now understand, doctor, why I'd rather have you on my side than with The Stygian?"

"You could have just left me alone. With the rest of the oblivious. I could have..."

"You couldn't have. They were getting closer. They needed you–or at least someone like you. That's why I needed to find you first. And I did."

"But..."

"I told you. I am a man of logic. I would have never interfered in your life if I had thought you to be insignificant. However, unfortunately you aren't." The writer finished, his grin evaporating off his face and leaving behind a more concerned expression.

"But what I cannot fathom..." Hemant finally spoke out, louder this time to avoid further interruptions from the writer "how anyone could possibly preserve antimatter here. Annihilation would be inevitable very soon after synthesis. Even the most advanced methods today, well those that are publicly disclosed, can only keep a very tiny amount of antimatter for up to 1000 seconds, which is just beyond an hour. So how? How, even with my apparently flawless plan..."

"Don't give yourself that much credit."

"Well, uh...even with my decent plan–is that alright, then?" The doctor asked, wearing a sarcastic expression.

"Perfect."

"How would The Stygian keep the antimatter 'fit and fine' long enough, so that they could purposefully initiate contact with its matter counterpart? Wouldn't the antimatter just disintegrate into raw energy before that?"

"Well, that's what this Obduratium is for." The writer suggested plainly. However, his eyes now remained fixated on the tiny door just behind the doctor and himself.

"What do you mean?" A perplexed Dr Shah enquired.

"Doctor, are you familiar with the applebox theory?" The writer asked casually, his eyes still fixated on the door.

"Uh...no...that can't...well..."

"Tell me doctor...what does the theory suggest?"

"If..."

"If...yes, go on."

"Well, if there were to be an indestructible box that could contain anything and everything, and if we were to put an object made up of a finite number of components—that object would exist in all its possible states infinitely...inside the box. Every possible state that could exist in that box—would exist." Hemant finished—unable to fully fathom what he himself had just let roll out of his tongue. His mind began racing, and as his eyes widened further, Hemant began glaring at the block of Obduratium.

"This...t-this Obduratium...this is...the-the indestructible box!" The doctor epiphanized. His hands for the first time shook slightly—his body had turned still.

"Precisely" The writer said, without looking away from the tiny door. "And if we were to store anti-alpha particles in this 'indestructible box'..."

"...the antimatter...could technically exist indefinitely." Hemant finished the writer's sentence, still in awe. "Even if some matter were to slip into the box, the annihilation would hardly matter. It would only be a matter of time before...before the produced energy reconstructed itself back into the respective antiparticles and particles. But...if this collision is supposed to release enough energy to wipe out the everyday people, then, how could this box withstand..."

"The Stygian aims to build thousands of these boxes—to distribute the antimatter in smaller amounts and store them safely. Of course, to do that they would need to extract that much Obduratium—and this one box is the only prototype...that's why they need it so badly. That's why I stole it. That's why we are about to be attacked in 3 seconds." The writer explained, his posture now in an athletic position, his feet planted to the aeroplane floor—his hands gently brushing against his sides, and his eyes now fixated on the door in an almost predatory fashion.

"Wow...that's brillia...wait what! Attack?" Before Hemant could think further, the door in front of them collapsed thunderously, polymerized chunks flying everywhere. Everything around Hemant had turned into a blurred mosaic of chaos. He could sense the dynamism of it all, the screeching noises, the pushing sensation, the smell of burnt plastic; however, he could not make absolute sense out of it. He felt his feet abandon the aeroplane floor, his body slowly being lifted into the air, his hands flailing in every direction like limp noodles—it was timeless. Hemant drifted through it all without really understanding what had happened.

Thud!

For the duration of a lonely second, everything had gone black, but then Hemant was slowly able to open his eyes. Now on the ground, right beside the huge block of Obduratium, Hemant realised that the door his companion kept looking at had exploded in their faces. Naturally, the eruptive force had propelled Hemant backwards, off the aeroplane floor, hurtling him into the Obduratium, beside which he now lay. Hemant was now surrounded with a dark, pungent smoke—that was tardily clearing away. As he felt around his body, he realised that he had not been terribly injured, feeling only a few bruises here and there. His clothes contrastingly had taken a horrific beating—his overcoat being riddled with scars of torn fabric, and his linen shirt and trousers being torn completely in certain areas.

As Hemant's senses slowly regained composure, he began hearing a yelping sound. Suddenly a flurry of concern and worry flooded Hemant's mind. He looked desperately trying to find his companion—the thick smoke only cleared out sparingly.

"Quilton? Quilton!" Hemant yelled into the void of smoke, which had now dissociated to a great extent, yet Hemant's eyes still betrayed him in finding the writer. However, Hemant's concern had promptly been shot dead, when a voice, unlike the one that made the yelping noise, with equal octaves of gruff and melody reached out to him assuringly.

"Doctor, are you alright?" It called out to him, and as Hemant slowly got back to his feet, he finally saw it. A horrific yet mesmerising view it was. The writer stood there. That feral look within his eyes had completely overtaken his demeanour, and his face had transfigured into a brooding beast-like expression. His body was surprisingly relaxed, his skin sweat-free, his stance unwavering and unshaking. His eyes remained fixated on an armed man with a padded black uniform, who continued to yelp in slow, painful agony. Hemant saw the armed man dangling, his feet above the aeroplane floor, his neck clasped tightly by the writer's hands, his face contorting inhumanly, exhibiting the uncanny affliction that he felt. A huge assault rifle lay idol beneath the dangling man, which Hemant imagined the writer to have strategically placed when disarming the armed man. The man continued to yelp as he choked at the hands of the writer–whose expression remained cold, and beast-like.

"ADDAMS! What are you doing, man? Get a hold of yourself! You'll...you'll kill him!" Hemant yelled slowly drawing closer to his companion, unable to think of an appropriate response to this bizarre situation.

"That's the plan, doctor. That's always been the plan." The writer responded icily. "It's funny...you now know very well that Quilton Addams is not my real name, yet you still chose to call me that in a moment of distress."

"You can't kill him! Don't bloody do this! You can't do this, Addams. You hear me!" Hemant yelled even louder. He frantically looked around; however, he could see nothing but the horrific sight in front of him. The remaining smoke from the minor explosion still hid everything else in view like overdrawn curtains.

"Can't I?" The writer asked without looking away from the yelping man. "Doctor, he was about to do the same to us. You realise, he's already sold himself to The Stygian. He's not an innocent man. If there's no innocence, then there's no loss, innit?" The writer mockingly asked the yelping man, who coughed even louder now as the writer's grip grew tighter around his neck. At the moment all Hemant could do was watch. His body had completely betrayed him, as it failed to move. He was stranded there, left to watch this strange, cold and calculated brutality from a man, whom he never expected to be so detached from humanity.

"Y-you khwacggk–ewarfph!" The yelping man began in a very raspy tone, trying to speak through his deathly coughs and yelps. "Y-you're–ewarfph eghaphf! You're a dead man–khwacggk erf egahphf! Dead, you hear me, bloody quiller!"

"Ah. Doctor...that's it. You know now. Quiller. That's what they call me." The writer plainly said before gently twisting his wrist. The armed man choked out his last breath, before falling to the floor–his body as lifeless as a brick. Hemant simply stood there unable to process the gruesomeness of the situation. The writer simply looked at him remorselessly.

"You...y-you killed him. It was so easy for you." Hemant began, but his words reached only deaf ears, and nothing more.

"He was a ruthless criminal. His time in the marine corps he spent spreading violence and dread overseas in poorer countries. And worst of all he enjoyed it. I knew this man. In fact, I know a lot of them. They're remotely not good people, doctor."

"And you are?"

"No. I'm a terrible person. But I don't enjoy what I do. It's logic that drives me, not pleasure. And c'mon, you're a doctor–you've seen deaths, this should not scare you. Why are you traumatised, doctor?"

"But you just...I...how?" Hemant murmured; his eyes fixated on the limp body in black padded uniform in front of him.

"You know Shah, I know what's scaring you. It's not death–no, with your medical experience you've been exposed to all that. And you're not scared of me..."

"No, I think I am. You're...you're a monster. I've never met a person so outlandish and downright cruel as you...but that doesn't seem to matter...because—because you seem to justify everything you do as logical reasoning. If someone's good, you use them, if someone's bad you kill them. That's not logic...that's just lack of emotion. You're just as bad as..." Hemant said blankly, suddenly coming to an abrupt halt before completing his sentence. His vision still fluttered over the still body of the black uniformed guard.

The pungent smoke had cleared out completely by now, and soon Hemant realised that they were faced by hundreds of armed men in jet-black uniforms pointing their rifles at him and the Quiller. In addition to the army of men in black, stood a masked man with a golden monocle attached to the right side of his mask, and nothing for his left. By now Hemant knew who this man was. A high-ranking official of the elite underground organisation known as The Stygian–his code name being The Feint. His hands remained pocketed in his slick, black trench coat, his left foot resting on top of an injured James Rex.

"Oi!" The detective cried out, miniscule streams of blood oozing out of his mouth, tainting his perfectly groomed beard, and perfectly tailored clothing. "If you lot are done with your bloody honeymoon...then I could use some help here." He croaked. Hemant noticed the detective's eyes flashing with outrage. Of course, a man of his metal was not afraid. The detective was simply angered that he could not hold off this Tartarean task force for long enough.

"Doctor...Hemant...Shah." The masked man broke out at a whispery register. "You could have helped me. You could have prevented...this damnation...this chaos that you've brought unto yourself."

"And then what? Die with the rest of them? You were going to kill off the regular blokes like us, anyway, right?" Hemant growled, an estranged sense of malice reuniting with him once more. As the doctor glared at The Feint, he realised that he was no longer afraid. He was angry. He was contemptuous. But fear failed to inject itself into Hemant's conscience–failed even at the sight of this savage devil that The Feint was.

"Oho!" The Feint sniggered loudly. "So, the imbecile has disclosed the *big plan,* is it? Well, I guess you are right, doctor. I don't really care about you–but that way people are much better off, you know? No one...likes to be under my surveillance...constantly. I mean look at your idiot friend here..."

"He's not my friend!" Hemant spoke out abruptly, which surprised him the most. The Quiller withdrew his glance away from Hemant, and began glaring at The Feint. His fingers wrapped around each other tighter–to strengthen his fists. Hemant could once more find that feral, predatory look in his companion's eyes.

"Well...friend, comrade, frenemy–whatever you want to call it–I don't really give a..." The Feint stopped himself promptly. He looked down at the detective who scowled back at him, more blood spewing out of his mouth. Hemant could now clearly see the true extent to which James Rex's face had been scarred and mangled. His clothes were also torn in several areas, and cuts and folds around the fabric of his clothing exposed several newly made bruises and scars on his body.

"Blimey...I...I forgot about you for a second, detective." The Feint began once more, his left foot slowly digging deeper into the detective's chest. "Well, excuse my language...but your idiot friend has been running away from me for ages, doctor! And now he's dragged you into this. Tsk Tsk Tsk." The masked man finished, his foot diving further into the detective's chest.

"ARRGh!" Cried out the detective as the sudden pain introduced itself with unmatched velocity. Hemant's glance quickly shifted back to the detective, sweat droplets accumulated at the surface of his forehead due to the sheer distress of the moment.

"Oh. Did I get the sternum then, Rex? I'll have to check if my shoe left an imprint...later." The Feint joked maliciously, before sniggering loudly. The detective continued to croak in pain, his eyes sharply exhibiting an amalgamation of anguish and anger.

"Stop!" Hemant yelled, unable to think of anything else to say to the deranged masked man. His body began shaking once more, his face now metamorphosed into a pool of nervous sweat. He quickly glanced at his other companion, who simply stood there, unemotive, staring at the tragedy unfolding.

"Do something! Why, you're the master of all fighting styles, right? That's what you told me in that damned café, remember? Stop them! Stop them!" Hemant yelled louder, his eyes moving around rapidly in their sockets. During this flurry of a moment, Hemant caught a quick glimpse of the other passengers, now glued to their seats–pure terror exhibited on their faces. The doctor knew that now it was all at the hands of the lesser of the two evils. If this was to be stopped, only the Quiller could do so. If not, then along with the detective and the several innocent passengers, Hemant was to meet his demise at the hands of The Stygian.

"I'm not a monster, doctor." The Quiller spoke suddenly, catching Hemant completely off-guard. "I'm simply ahead of the curve." He finished plainly. The feral look in his eyes had reached flash point, and his body had transfigured itself into a neat, and composed posture. It was only the Quiller's face that told a tale. If emotion was disadvantageous to the Quiller, then at this moment he was the most disadvantaged, for Hemant could feel the purity of the fury spewing out of the Quiller.

Suddenly, a distinct click of a button was audible to Hemant, evidently originating from the Quiller's right hand that hid itself behind his back, and the next second all the armed guards started shaking and groaning. Promptly, Hemant realised that it was the huge rifles and automatic armed weapons that had undergone a malfunction, and now were somehow electrocuting the armed men holding them. The next moment, without warning, the Quiller suddenly leapt at The Feint, twisting mid-air to commit to a spin kick. His left foot collided with The Feint's right elbow, which had been hastily lifted to block the sudden death blowing kick. Nevertheless, the abrupt move from the Quiller knocked The Feint off the detective's body and he stumbled a few steps backwards, before staggering to his knees to thwart himself from falling down. Instinctively, Hemant grabbed onto the detective's body, and pulled him aside.

"Get to the pilot's cabin. You'll find the resources there. Get the detective up and ready as soon as possible." The Quiller yelled as he squared The Feint, and the now fallen guards, who had dropped the weapons and staggered to the aeroplane floor like their commander.

"But what about you? What about the Obduratium?" Hemant wheezed, as he pulled on the detective's body with all his might.

"Go! Now." were the only words that came out of the Quiller's mouth. Determined to not waste any more time, Hemant yanked the detective's body off the floor with great difficulty, balancing the inspector's body onto his own shoulders, before briskly running to the other end of the aeroplane.

As Hemant ran, he realised that he was stepping over multiple bodies, all of which belonged to other armed men in black uniforms whom the detective had managed to successfully *neutralise*. About 50 unconscious bodies simply lay there on Hemant's path to the pilot's cabin. Hemant glanced back at the detective who was limping by Hemant's side–his body completely dependent on Hemant's shoulders.

"Not bad, eh?" The detective said as he grinned smugly, revealing a mangled, broken set of teeth, with large gaping gaps here and there. The doctor could only stare back in awe, impressed by the determination of the man he now carried. Soon they reached the pilot's cabin–where they found all of the crew tied with a tight, thick fibre. After gently placing the detective's body on the aeroplane floor, Hemant quickly untied the pilot and co-pilot, along with the other stewards and stewardesses. Several of them were still unconscious, and remained lifelessly on the floor. Hemant yelled to the other conscious crew members to bring him all the medical kits available on flight, before alerting the members of the current scenario. The cabin crew was barely injured, which told Hemant that this Feint was not fond of the idea of wasting bullets or energy. The cabin crew of this flight was simply too insignificant, Hemant figured, for The Feint to really care about them. Hemant demanded the crew members to stay vigilant and grab hold of any item that could be utilised as a weapon to defend oneself. Amidst the panic, the crew members had no other option but to follow the doctor's lead.

Hemant knew he couldn't lock the cabin doors. Several innocent passengers still remained at their seats–terrified of the ongoing ruckus that continued to unfold within the aeroplane corridors. However, this Tartarean task force seemed to be focused on the Quiller and the Obduratium, and so the passengers were likely safer without Hemant or anyone else interfering.

"Your form is terrible just as always, Quill." The masked man with a golden monocle for his right eye said, as he sneered at the Quiller getting pummelled by three black-suited guards. Promptly, however, the Quiller squatted to the floor and knocked down all three guards with an extended leg sweep. The guards fell to the floor brilliantly, creating a loud thud that echoed throughout the aeroplane corridor. All the remaining passengers remained as quiet as possible–mothers clasping their hands tightly onto their toddlers' mouths, older folks shivering quietly in their seats, youthful men and women silently watching in awe and fear, as the short breadth of life that they had lived flashed before their eyes–all passengers tried to draw the least amount of attention to themselves. However, it was evident that the Quiller had strengthened their last strand of hope, and they believed that there was still a chance of safety.

"Just as always you're standing at the back–while your men try to do the work for you." The Quiller began, punching one of the few remaining conscious guards with a devastating liver shot, and then finishing off the last guard with a spinning hook kick to the jaw. The guards fell to the floor like stacks of dominoes, lifeless upon hitting the ground.

"Not today, mate." The Quiller finished. He stared The Feint dead in the monocle, and was met with a similar stare in return.

"You...really think you're...ready? Ready for me, Quilly?" The masked man jeered. He looked at the Quiller and then he playfully glanced at the other terrified passengers of the plane.

"You want the Obduratium. Come and..."

"No, I...want to kill YOU! The Order...wants the Obduratium." The Feint began interrupting the Quiller. "And just to make this interesting...if *you*...don't kill *me*, then all of these people...well, erm, let's just say they would never see the light of day again." Said the masked man with a monocle, pointing a finger at the several terrified passengers–some of whom had now begun wailing, screaming, and chanting morbidly in terror and fear–behind him and the Quiller.

"You wouldn't do that." The Quiller said plainly, however, it was evident that a tinge of nervousness had struck him for the first time in a very long time.

"Wouldn't I?" The Feint asked mockingly. "I...am not a man of logic, Quilly. I am a man of obsession–and I'm most obsessed with hurting you–especially after you messed things up for me by stealing that Obduratium."

"Your gatekeepers were incompetent. Not my fault."

"Enough chit-chat. If you don't–erm–well...if you don't *neutralise* me, then these people will die. And THAT...will be on YOU!" The Feint said threateningly, a menacing aura taking over his atmosphere. The Quiller slowly glanced at the terrified passengers. These were the people. These were the people who needed protection the most. These were the people The Stygian sought to destroy. This was the reason *he*...wanted to destroy The Stygian. Suddenly a new fury ignited within the Quiller, and for the very first time–he felt as though he cared. He cared about the innocent passengers on the plane. That was not logic. That was impulse...instinct; and the Quiller...he was ready.

Within moments the two individuals leapt at each other. A manic aura danced in the air around them, and as they embarked on this ruthless battle, the passengers watched in awe a legendary encounter.

"You feeling alright?" Hemant asked the detective, who now attempted to slowly get back to his feet. The pilot's cabin had not been interrupted by any ruckus for a prolonged amount of time. Almost all of the cabin crew were now conscious, untied, and in their senses. The pilots had no choice but to continue flying the aircraft even through the fear and panic. They had already informed the transponder of the strange hijack that had occurred and now were heading for the nearest airport–the Lynden Pindling International Airport in Bahamas.

"Yeah. We need to go back out there." The detective responded as he looked out the cabin door. The heap of unconscious armed men had only grown bigger since they abandoned the back of the Aeroplane. He looked back at the crew, who seemed to give him and the doctor an encouraging look, and a few stewards even declared their desire to help. The detective, like the doctor, thought it better to go alone and not risk the lives of anyone else.

"There're already several innocent passengers in imminent danger. It would be more helpful if all of you remain here and tend to them as we send them here. Stay vigilant and stay calm." Hemant announced before exiting the cabin with the detective and gently closing it without making a sound. As they carefully crept through the corridor, determined to not make a single noise, they approached the passengers one by one–alerting them to stay quiet and ushering them back to the front of the plane. It took the duo a few minutes before they ushered all the passengers towards the front of the plane, making sure that there was enough distance between them and the area that was now guarded with several unconscious men in black uniform on the ground. The doctor and detective knew what their next task was. It had been a while since they left their companion behind. The two slowly crept closer to the back of the plane, before they finally saw it.

The Feint stood there looking nearly untouched–sparing a few cuts along the folds of his expensive fabric. The only thing visibly destroyed was the man's mask, which seemed to have been torn in half, exposing a mangled set of bleeding lips and a nose that breathed heavily. Besides this minute damage, The Feint appeared fine. His posture was confident and calm, and his exposed mangled lips now wore a terrible grin. The Feint was now looking down at the Quiller, who had been injured much worse. Strands of hair had been torn out from his scalp, his face bleeding and as mangled as his adversary's. His body exhibited much more damage, however, than his counterpart–riddled with cuts and gashes along his strange mediaeval ensemble, which now drooped open to expose even larger scars and bruises on his body. He was breathing very heavily, as he attempted to get up. Promptly, The Feint grabbed the Quiller and kneed him in the abdomen. The Quiller huffed loudly, his eyes watering as the stinging pain registered. Quickly pushing away The Feint, he staggered to the floor once more before slowly getting up again.

"Arrghh!" The Quiller yelled as he threw a powerful haymaker at The Feint's face, yet the now partially masked man simply smiled and dodged the punch effortlessly, weaving to the side and unleashing a powerful liver shot that made the Quiller cough out a few droplets of blood. The Quiller stumbled backwards and The Feint simply stood there smiling; however, determined to hit his target, the Quiller began unleashing a series of death-blowing kicks–first a push kick, followed by a roundhouse, before a side kick, and finally an axe kick–all of which The Feint avoided efficaciously, before countering the Quiller's final axe kick with a deafening side kick that seemed to break a rib or two out of the Quiller's rib cage.

"Ahh!" The Quiller yelled as he staggered back to the floor, this time unable to get up. He looked at The Feint with relentless hate; however, his body had suddenly given up on him–feeling the sharp pain rise from his rib-cage all the way to his head, the Quiller simply sat there gazing hatefully at his adversary.

As the detective and doctor slowly drew close to the scene, they noticed all the idol weapons lying around. They glanced at each other and then nodded. The detective steadily and quietly picked up an automatic rifle off the ground, and began examining the ammunition within the weapon.

"Do you now realise–why...I let my men do the fighting? You could easily defeat them. It was fun to watch. But now...well, you can say for yourself, can you not?" The Feint mocked the Quiller before sighing. "Well, this was fun...and you–you fought very well, Quilly, I must say. But...I'm...*me*, and you're only *you*. And you know, no one can really defeat *me*."

"I would think twice, if I were you!" Yelled the detective before firing the rifle in his hand, pointing the gun directly at The Feint's shoulder.

"Arghhh!" The Feint yelled as he briskly turned around. His face now looked even more battle damaged, as more blood gently leaked out of his nose and his mouth—while fresh crimson liquid began oozing out of the newly made bullet wound by virtue of the detective. He glared at the doctor and the detective like a mad animal, and for the first time Hemant truly saw the cold, icy exterior of the masked man abandoned him, leaving behind something even more ruthless, primal, and manic. Suddenly, The Feint ran towards the duo without warning, ready to leap and attack; however, the detective—with trained reflexes of a brilliant policeman—quickly shot two more rounds of bullets at the chest of the battled damaged monster that had begun running towards him.

"Yarghh...Arfhgh!" The Feint finally yelped before stumbling to his knees right in front of the doctor and the detective. "Bullets...haha...bullets are not going to stop me! Bullets aren't going to stop The Stygian!" The Feint continued yelling before roaring with a menacing laughter. Hemant was so taken aback by the lunatic laughter he distanced himself from the man with three sets of bullet wounds now in his systems, kneeling down shaking with angsty laughter. The doctor and the detective, unable to determine their next move, were suddenly met with a jump-scare from the Quiller, who had managed to leap onto The Feint, and grab him in a choke-hold. The Quiller then dragged the partially masked man—who could still barely stop laughing—and while choking him, began kneeing him constantly around the abdomen. The feral look had overtaken the Quiller's expression once more and as he dragged The Feint to the edge of an emergency exit, he fastened himself to the nearby handle by his strange, serpentine belt—and then...proceeded to open the gates.

The doctor and the detective quickly grabbed onto nearby seats, before an immense amount of force began pulling everything outwards—outside the aeroplane. The Quiller stood there tightly fastened to the nearby handle by his trusty belt, his hands clinging onto The Feint–whose feet were now dangling and wobbling outside the aeroplane.

"You know very well…" The Feint began, his voice unusually calm for someone who had been shot and was now partially dangling out of an aeroplane that was still midair. "…if you don't kill me now, I will come back much worse. I will keep coming back to haunt you–if you don't end me, now!"

"Well," The Quiller sighed. "That's the plan." His hands promptly let go of the bleeding, torn, laughing man, who simply flew out of the aeroplane with a maniacal smile on his face. A few seconds later, the Quiller simply closed the emergency door, and unfastened himself again. The doctor and the detective ran to him to support him in standing up.

"We haven't got enough stuff to fix you right now. How did it get this bad?" Hemant asked, unable to hide the tone of concern seeping through into his voice.

"It's alright, doctor. Rex…still got that coin?" The Quiller asked as he slowly began stumbling back to the block of Obduratium.

"The coin? You know…about…that?" The detective asked, as he explicitly expressed his astonishment.

"Brother…" The Quiller began, a wide boyish grin returning back to the composition of his face "I planted it there. For you to have."

"Bullocks. I really thought I was on to something there." The detective said earnestly. "Well, there you go." He finished as he fetched the coin out of a pocket in his trousers and tossed it to the Quiller. The distinct clink of the coin being tossed rang out rather loudly, however, Hemant found himself appreciating the sweet harmony within the sound.

"Also…detective, help me out and fix the people here, will ya?" The Quiller said airily as he observed the coin with a giant capital B.

"*Fix them*…what do you mean?" Hemant began, but before he could elaborate upon his question, it was already answered.

"They don't need to remember us, do they?" The detective suggested. "Right. Will the Blursion do?"

"No!" The Quiller exclaimed. "We're not trying to kill them—they're innocent. Plus, you gave enough trouble with that when you made that mess in the Hospital."

"So, you did kill the Alverez brothers?" Hemant inquired, shooting a disapproved look to the detective.

"That's entirely another story." The detective said, swiftly ignoring Hemant's claims. "Then I'm using the Pretermittus Spray...quick and easy."

"Fine." The Quiller said, as he slowly placed the block of Obduratium in front of the same emergency door, through which he had expelled a battle-scarred, partially masked, and hysterically laughing Feint, moments ago.

"And what? This-this will just erase their memories" Hemant inquired, visibly tired of the wacky, uncharted gadgets and instruments that the detective and the Quiller kept pulling out of their pockets.

"No." The detective said frankly, and without saying anything else, and without waiting to entertain any other comment from Hemant he simply walked off to the front of the aeroplane.

"Well, doctor...we still have some time left. Let's disarm this *weapon of mass destruction*, shall we?" The Quiller said abruptly.

"Hemant glanced at the Obduratium block once, before looking at the Quiller and saying "It's an empty box, no? What's there to...erm...disarm?"

The Quiller smiled briefly, his gaze still focused on the coin, as he began. "Shah. As long as it's useful to The Stygian, it's dangerous."

"Right- the 'coming back to haunt you' dilemma. No, I get it. So, what do we do?" Hemant asked casually. For a moment the Quiller said nothing. Then, abruptly picking up the Obduratium block and turning it horizontally by 180 degrees, the Quiller faced the doctor, revealing a circular padlock on the Obduratium box. Then he took the golden coin with a giant capital B as its logo, and placed it securely onto the padlock. The coin matched the padlock perfectly, and remained fastened to it. Hemant continued to look at this strange procedure, devoting all his attention to the distinct steps the Quiller followed. After making sure that the coin had become a part of the Obduratium box, the Quiller turned the coin, which had now turned into a make-shift dial, thrice–waiting a few seconds after each turn to proceed to the next. After doing so, he simply waited. Nothing happened. The Quiller's eyes remained fixated on the makeshift dial, Hemant's eyes being fixated on the Quiller, and they waited for a few more minutes. Nothing still.

"Oh." The Quiller spoke suddenly. "I...thought..."

"Don't you know how this works?" Hemant asked airily, not expecting much, however, he suddenly realised that his companion was looking rather dumbfounded. Hemant looked at the Quiller curiously, before looking back at the Obduratium box.

"I thought there'd be some holographic keypad that would pop up." The Quiller said, his confusion evident in his eyes.

"How'd you figure that?" The doctor asked, a streak of curiosity flashing amidst his expression.

"Well, I'd found out that the lock system of this box fostered an electric switch *without* a battery or a cell. I just assumed that this coin contained the concealed battery, and once it was completely fastened to the box, and connected to the switch it would produce a current, which would either open the box, or put forward a keypad, or something like that." The Quiller finished, still visibly dumbfounded by the anomaly he had failed to expect. Suddenly a strange idea flashed in front of Hemant's eyes. He could feel his imagination stirring something creative, until his mind had finally put forward a thought that he himself was too incredulous to believe. However, being in a situation, where someone claiming to be ingenious at every field of human endeavour was himself stunned, Hemant had to try out his way.

"And...and you're certain, that this lock system has a concealed circuit within?" Hemant asked as a jovial smile erupted across his face. The Quiller simply nodded, still completely taken aback by the fact that he had made an error. Wasting no time, Hemant kneeled in front of the box and drew his hand closer to the makeshift dial. He gripped it exactly the way he had observed the Quiller to have done. Then instead of turning the dial in the singular clockwise direction like the Quiller, Hemant began turning it clockwise and anticlockwise alternatively. Promptly the lid of the box snapped backwards to reveal the empty space inside the container. Hemant smiled as he slowly got back to his feet.

"How'd you do that?" The Quiller asked, evidently astonished by the doctor's brilliance.

"You were just off because of one singular judgement, man!" Hemant explained as he gleamed at his companion. "It wasn't a circuit. It was a coil...and the coin is a magnet. Rotating the dial clockwise and anticlockwise continuously produced a changing magnetic field, which induced a current in the coil, which in turn...uh...I can only imagine, moved the springs of the lock in a certain way that it unlocked the box." Hemant suggested, as a triumphant mask took over his face. The Quiller was now smiling at his companion, evidently impressed by Hemant's quick thinking.

"So, if I were to just hammer this coin, it would disrupt the domains within its magnet, which would render the coin useless, and therefore the box to be useless as well." The Quiller epiphanized, as he removed the coin from the padlock of the Obduratium box once more.

"Precisely." Hemant responded as he comfortably sat down on a nearby seat. The next few minutes were spent in silence. The Quiller had busied himself in hammering and practically destroying the coin, before tossing a mauled and now nonfunctional coin back into the Obduratium box, and closing it. The doctor simply looked outside, waiting for both of his companions to finish their respective endeavours. The afternoon sky looked clear and bright. A few white clouds drifted here and there, revealing dashes of bright blue sky in between.

"Thank you, doctor." The Quiller suddenly spoke. "Without your calculative and calm composure–I would have probably died today, and I would have taken Rex's life, and the lives of all the other innocent passengers with me; because alone, I could have never saved them."

Hemant tried to think of something to say, something that would sum up this journey, this adventure that was now over. However, he could not bring himself to say anything. He simply smiled at the Quiller.

"Alright. Done." The detective howled as he casually walked back to the doctor and the Quiller. "We ready to go?"

"Go...where?" Hemant asked drearily, as he got up slowly from his seat again.

"Just try not to scream too loud doctor, eh?" The Quiller said briefly.

"Scream...what do you m..." Hemant began, however, before he could even finish his sentence, the Quiller suddenly got up and fastened the block of Obduratium to his belt with a strange harness, before swiftly opening the emergency door again.

"AAAARHHHHHHH!" Hemant cried as he felt his body being dragged out of the plane, the detective and the Quiller zooming past him in the open sky. All three of them free-falled, getting closer and closer to the vast ocean beneath. As Hemant screamed, he felt air whip him across the face. His hands and feet flailed around uncontrollably, while the detective and the Quiller smoothly made their way further below– getting even more closer to the surface of the ocean. Before Hemant could muster up enough courage to fix his posture and somehow get closer to his other two companions, his vision gave in–slowly metamorphosing into a blur...and soon enough, all Hemant saw was darkness, again.

CHAPTER XVI

The Magical Map

It was a beautiful evening in Tahiti beach, Bahamas. The sand was less reflective of the scorching heat, and the sun prepared itself to set near to a series of valleys in the distant mountains of another minor island. A late breeze kissed any and all surfaces in the surroundings, and as the tropical trees rustled cheerily, a particular trio consisting of a writer, a detective, and a doctor, sat in wooden chairs in a local shack, facing the sea and sipping on extravagant, tropical cocktails. A huge golden box lay on the wooden table in front of them, along with a large, blank piece of paper. The shack was bustling with a cheerful crowd, most of the people being drawn into a half drunken state, thanks to the delectable cocktails. A soft rock hymn with elements of jazz played in the background, originated from a chunky, rusty old speaker behind the bar. A few people sat at the bar watching the bartender do fabulous finger tricks with his glasses, bottles and mixers, while a few people sank their heads deep into the wooden surface of the bar–completely lost in a sleepy, drunken state.

"I...still can't believe...that colliding with the concrete waves of the ocean did not damage me whatsoever." Hemant began as he gazed at the light-blue sky, while sipping at his lime-coloured drink "D'you know they it hurts more to fall into the ocean than to fall onto land?"

"But you had that force-field around you, didn't you mate?" The detective promptly retorted, without shifting his glance away from the marvellous waves that rolled on top of each other. The Quiller simply smiled, and took a sip from his drink.

"What? N-no! There wasn't!" Hemant huffed in outrage. The detective looked astonished, and suddenly glanced at the Quiller. The Quiller just kept on smiling. The hymn had grown even louder now, and the sweet sea breeze only made the atmosphere more comforting.

"You didn't? Wait—seriously?" The detective demanded suddenly sharing the doctor's outrage. "He could have died! Are you..."

"Of course, I did. He would have been nearly dead in that explosion otherwise, detective." The Quiller whispered airily. "It was when I grabbed you by the arm, doctor. Remember?"

"Not really, if I'm bein' honest." Hemant said earnestly, as he lifted his shirt sleeve to examine his arm. There it was, a tattooed design that matched exactly the branded logo on the Quiller's trench coat. The Quiller simply nodded as Hemant glanced back at him, to suggest that this strange tattoo had indeed unleashed a forcefield around the doctor during the time of free fall into the vast seas near to the Island of Bahamas. Uninterested in the science of it all, the doctor simply took another sip from his lime drink and stared at the sea waves.

"You didn't quiet register me slapping the forcefield initiator onto your arm, because you were under the influence of the Phylocourd." Quiller said smiling, as he looked at the detective. "Remember? The Phylocourd that 'Mr Inspector', over here, forced down your throat?"

"Speaking of..." Hemant began once more staring at the detective.

"*Well*...erm...don't you want to ask our friend here, why he involved us into the matter, when he had the bloody box with him all this while?" The detective said hastily, quickly shifting the focus of the conversation in order to avoid getting verbally slammed by the doctor for overdosing him with the psychedelic antidote. The trick successfully worked, and Hemant began piercing Quiller with a look that demanded answers.

"You had the coin, man. What could I have done?" Quiller said swiftly, his boyish grin persisting over his face.

"No, you planted that coin...*remember*?" Hemant stated sarcastically, and this time his point was rallied for by the detective.

"Point to Shah!" The detective spat out as he grinned at the Quiller. "You planted that funky piece on my crime scene, remember? You could have bloody used it to do what you finally ended up doing on the darn plane!"

"Uhgh..." The Quiller sighed. His smile, however, continued to persist. "Can I just say...I was lonely, and leave it at that?" He asked jokingly.

The doctor and the detective gave out a chuckle in unison. For a moment they all glanced at the beach, taking in the mesmerising beauty of tropical nature.

"No, seriously, mate;" Hemant spoke out suddenly. "Why'd you secretly organise all this and drag us into it?"

"Well..." The Quiller began, and for a moment the detective felt as though he had noticed a deliberate tone of pride in the Quiller's voice. "I actually was stumped. I actually couldn't figure what that big lard of golden 'chunky' was until much later. Around that time, I had only known that the coin and the box were prototypes for a most renowned discovery The Stygian had made, and of course that meant that they were prototype devices that could help the *Extermination* process. I knew I had to steal them and destroy them. That's why I required the doctor's assistance, for I could tell—which you've rightfully proven today, Shah—that you harbour a massive intellect for not medical science and chemistry alone, but also in the fields of mechanics, and physics. I figured that you too, detective, knowing the ends and outs of The Stygian, and being able to sense the most miniscule shifts in your environment, would be of amazing assistance, and that's why I entrusted you with keeping the coin—just to make sure that the box and the coin were separated, so that The Stygian would have a harder time looking for them, once they were notified of the theft. I knew that next I had to plan a meeting for both of you, so that you could unite and start seeking me. A few strange letters to the detective were enough to target his excitement for working this job again, even though it had been a while since our last...project. For the doctor, I just upped the dosage of Dellirictus, which of course made you more jumpy, more curious, more insistent in doing what you wanted to do, and of course stranger—strange enough for the detective to notice you. I imagined that upon finding the detective in the hospital, you would begin asking him questions, after which he would realise that you both had a common associate—me. However, what I didn't expect was for him to mistake you for me, and then attack you, thinking that it was me, who was playing this role of a doctor just to toy with him, even though it was actually you telling the truth, doctor...so, uh.... thanks Rex." The Quiller took a moment to breathe, and the detective guiltily looked away, focusing only on his drink and the view beyond the shack.

"It was only later, that I was notified of the fact..." The Quiller began once more. "...that The Stygian had been using a certain, prominent Mob boss called Boccioni, who was collecting nuclear waste from all the factories in New York that were under his belt. Then...it took me little time to connect the dots. However, it was already too late...the coin was now with you, detective, so I had no choice, but to let my plan unfold just as it was. I needed you both to meet me on the plane. We would swiftly destroy the coin and the box, and then we would land in Hell's Kitchen—where are next plan of action would unfold. However, this last part was ruined by The Feint and his Tartarean task force, who decided to hijack the plane, kill me, and retrieve their beloved artefacts back. Thanks to you both, I was able to stop them, and thanks to you, Shah, I was able to effectively destroy this box. Because, for some unknown reason many months ago, if I would have chosen to dissociate you from my work, and take it upon myself to destroy this box, then I would have been stuck, and The Stygian could have gotten to me before I could destroy the coin, and render the Obduratium box useless. So, basically—all in all—my brilliant plan of recruiting the detective, and recruiting you—Shah—to work with me coincided with my brilliant plan of destroying the mass destruction prototypes of The Stygian, and it all worked out in brilliant fashion. Might I add...uh, it was brilliant!"

"There's the narcissist, I know." The detective mumbled, as he smirked. Hemant looked dazed for a moment before sitting straight and asking another question.

"But then...why are we still carrying this box? If it's...you know...useless and all?"

"You never know, mate, when you're gonna need to use an impenetrable material." The Quiller responded, still smiling. "And, if you're still wonderin'...yes! I really couldn't have opened the box without you. I was really stumped...even on the plane."

Hemant stared at the Quiller for a good five minutes. He could have never imagined that the man, who he believed was a narcissistic, delusional, deranged psychopath was actually complimenting him. The Quiller suddenly seemed much more human. The thought came crashing down to Hemant, and he had to sit back down to accept the fact that his conscience had already allowed him to forgive the Quiller, even after all the things that Hemant had been put through.

"I thought you never made mistakes. I thought you were good at everything." The detective said in hushed tones, evidently trying to throw a jibe at his companion.

"What can I say, man? I just get a little emotional when it comes to The Stygian." The Quiller wheezed, as he chuckled.

"Well, uh, this has been great. But I think I would want to get back to London..." Hemant began, his eyes darting from the detective to the Quiller. They both smiled back.

"Haven't you changed your mind, doctor? Are you sure that you don't want to work with us?" The Quiller said as he pointed at a waiter and gestured for a menu card.

"I... well...yes. Perhaps you're not that bad of a person—crazy? Yes. But you wanted to save those people on the plane as much as I did and I respect you for that. And things have been interesting these past few months, except the fact that you were secretly breaking into my apartment and drugging me. I...well, to be honest I really don't know now. On one hand, I'm terrified that I'll encounter something much worse if I continue to work with you; on the other...I have started to get addicted to the adrenaline. I don't know, mate. I want to leave, but also, I want to stay."

"Well, you kinda have to be with us for a while anyway, mate. The Scotland Yard thinks you killed the Alverez brothers and they're sort of trying to hunt you down over there." Quiller interrupted abruptly. The detective had begun laughing loudly, and the doctor just looked flabbergasted.

"WHAT! You lot have labelled me a damn criminal! WHAT! Quiller, tell me you're joking!" Hemant yelled, utterly taken aback and even more outraged.

"I'll *tell* you our next plan of action, eh?" The Quiller said as he tapped his finger gently on the blank piece of paper. Suddenly, different hieroglyphics began appearing on the paper, which was then followed by strands of longitude and latitude marks that covered the paper like strings. Several written remarks, notes, and annotations, along with numbers that marked locations began appearing on the paper, and soon enough the blank paper now completely looked like a brilliant world map. Ignoring the doctor's awe, the Quiller proceeded to pinch on the illustrated continent of the United States, and as though a digital screen, the paper zoomed in on a very specific location–Hell's Kitchen.

"We need to go there. And then Bohemian Groves." The Quiller said, and the detective simply raised his glass in agreement. Hemant stared at the map for a few seconds before speaking once more.

"How'd you do that?" He asked earnestly, completely forgetting about the fact that he was now a wanted criminal in London.

"Magic!" The Quiller exclaimed casually.

"No really! How'd you..."

"I'm telling you, it's magic. The modern world may not believe in the mystic arts, but that don't mean it isn't real, doctor." The Quiller stated airily. "Remember the self-healing wounds on the Alverez brothers—oh and that mysterious air pocket in Eduardo Alverez's throat, which vanished automatically, after the man had collapsed?"

A waiter had finally brought out a menu card and the Quiller began looking through the items.

"We'll discuss this later, eh? I'm famished right now!" He said, his head remained lowered as he kept skimming through the several listed food items. Hemant saw the detective nod before leaning back and getting lost in his Pina Colada completely, and so Hemant realised that he had no choice but to comply. However, for some condemned, unknowable reason, this did not seem bad at all to the doctor. He glanced back at his companions and realised that his life had completely changed in the matter of a few months. He was no longer a part of the *Grey World*. He had tasted the exhilaration of the black and white for long enough; in London he was now known as a criminal, to The Stygian he was now a prominent adversary, and now there was no going back; and Hemant welcomed this shift in his reality with a concerned smile on his face and delicious lime drink in his hand.

"We've already met the black—the elite civilisation hell-bent on destroying the Grey World. It's time we meet the white—Bohemian Groves—that's where we'll find them, fellow reader. Stay tuned!"

Prelimenary Character Sketches

123